Rebecca Rose

Not Broken
Just Human

Art by Frankie Cornejo

Lunada Press, LLC

Lunada Press, LLC

ISBN 13: 978-0937176-01-6

To My Readers

"Not Broken, Just Human" contains content that might be troubling to some readers, including but not limited to, depictions of and references to cutting and self-harm, childhood trauma, death, suicide, and PTSD, inter alia. Please be mindful of these and other possible triggers and seek assistance if needed.

I do not believe depression will ever 'go away'. I know my own depression will always be with me, but I have learned depression doesn't have to consume every part of my life.

The first part of this book is about depression sneaking up on a person. Depression isn't always obvious, and this can cause denial and suppression of emotions. The second part of this book is about how depression can consume a person and sometimes even become one's personality. Sometimes it's just dark jokes that are a little too truthful.

In the third part of the book a depressed person starts to feel better, but it does not mean the person is cured. I have found depression will come back at inconvenient times. However, in my opinion, I believe that once you make depression just a part of you, and not the entirety of you, then you can start living life.

Depression will always be a struggle. But I hope that this book helps people in some way or another. Hopefully, my journey through this depression nightmare will have a positive outcome for my readers.

Art by QMKN Studio

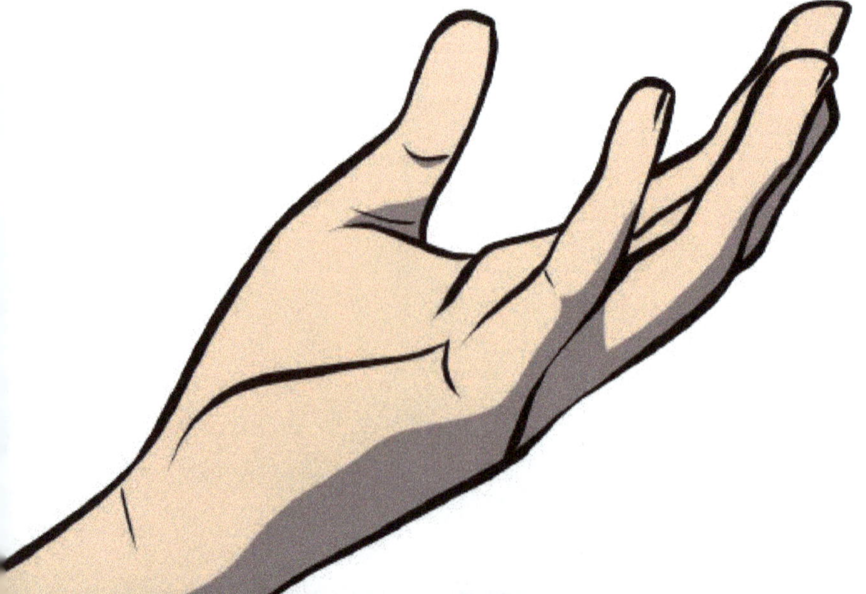

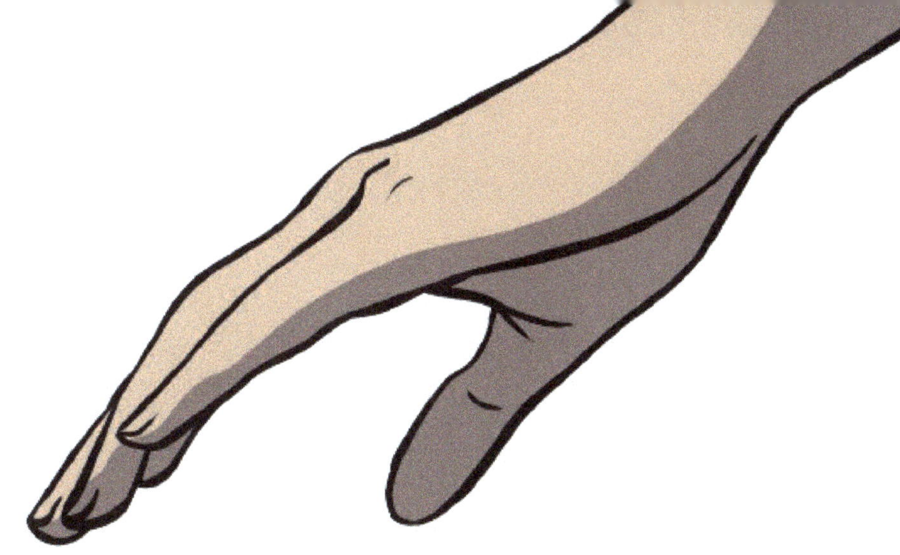

I
REFUSE
TO
CHANGE

I want to improve;
I want to get better.

However, I don't want to change.

A bold statement. Conflicting to some and confusing to others. Many misunderstand or can't comprehend. And yet, it is possible. First, let's start with the difference: improving means "become better," while changing means "become different."

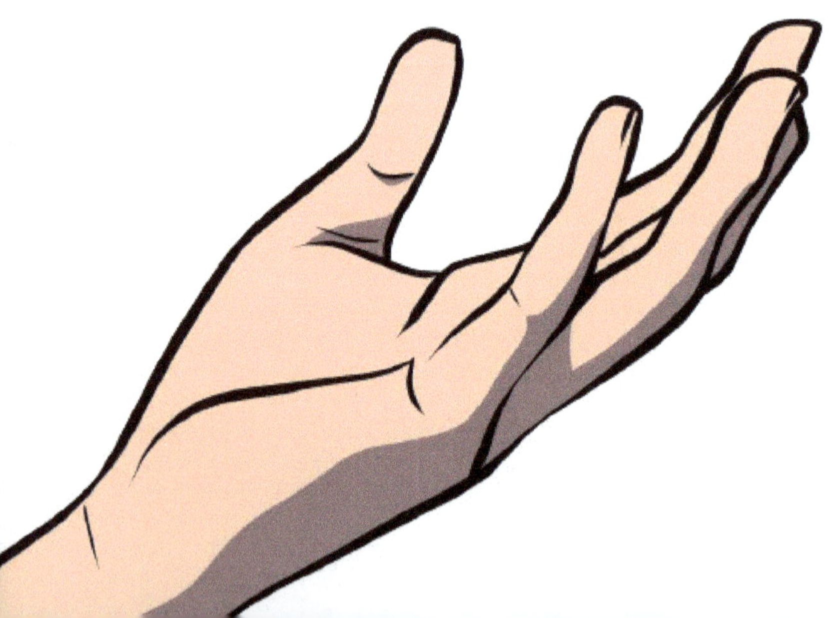

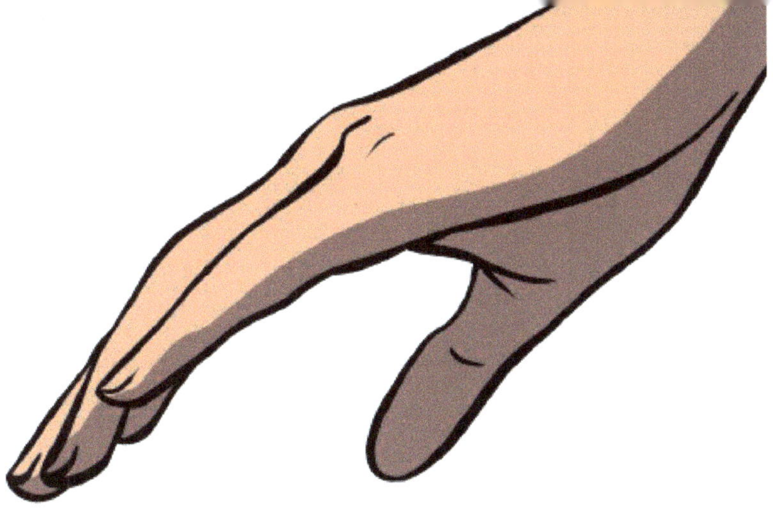

Like the author, Peter Drucker said in his book *Managing Oneself*, "Do not try to change yourself – you are unlikely to succeed. But work hard to improve the way you perform." Changing oneself is about becoming a different person, but "To be yourself in a world that is constantly trying to make you something else is the greatest accomplishment" (Emerson). Just because the world is constantly changing does not mean that we as human beings need to change. Instead, we need to improve, like a caterpillar upgrading into a butterfly. It is the same bug, made with the same DNA.

For example, therapy, to many means to change one's habits to improve one's life. However, I'd like to argue that instead, people need to improve their habits to improve their lives.

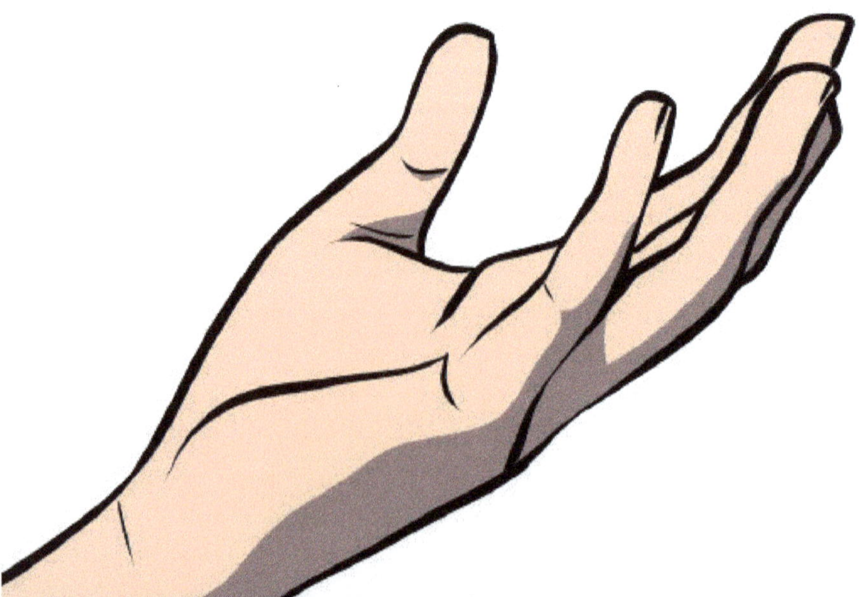

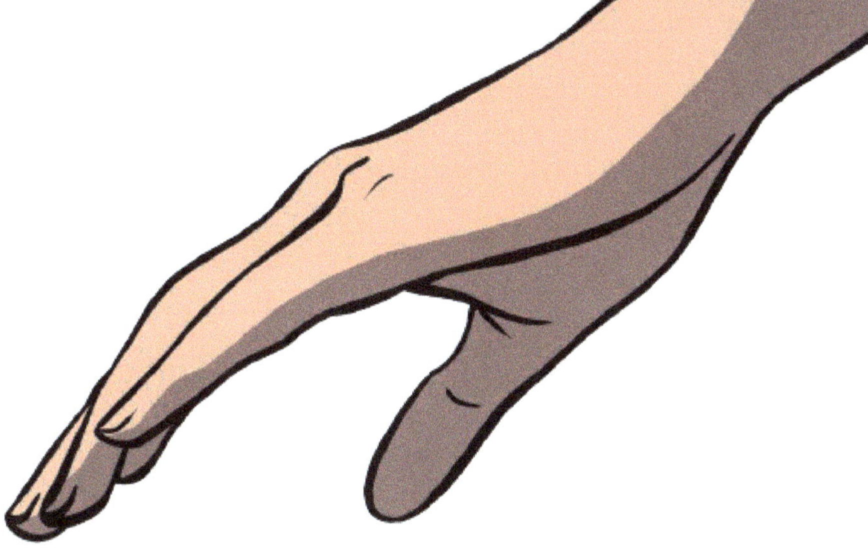

In therapy, a standard practice taught for clients to develop is changing their thoughts. Yet, I do this "change" by alternatively using my negative thoughts as fuel for writing poetry. This helps me challenge my thoughts and work through my intense and complex feelings. My thoughts will always be just that, thoughts! But I do have the ability to slowly evolve my thoughts into something more optimal. Actions need to be improved.

Don't Be
Needy

Don't be needy

Attention is for whores

They don't believe me

Every moment that passes by

Speeds my heart

It's exhausting

Air seeps out of my lungs

I no longer know how to breath

I don't seem to remember

Am I being dramatic?

Am I dying?

What is going on with me?

Bad memories tend to haunt me

I relive the past

Unable to remember the present

I fear the future

Wishing it won't come

My body has been acting strange

Little motivation to none

I don't know how to put the experiences into words

Without the ability to explain

I can't ask for help

I can't be dramatic

I can't overreact

I'm fine

Attention is only for whores

Everyone is already suffering

Suffering with something

In which there's no cure

Something that is worse

Than I could ever understand

Everyone has it worse than me

So, I ignore

I am fine

There's nothing wrong

I shouldn't ask for help

That's just asking for attention

Attention, I don't deserve

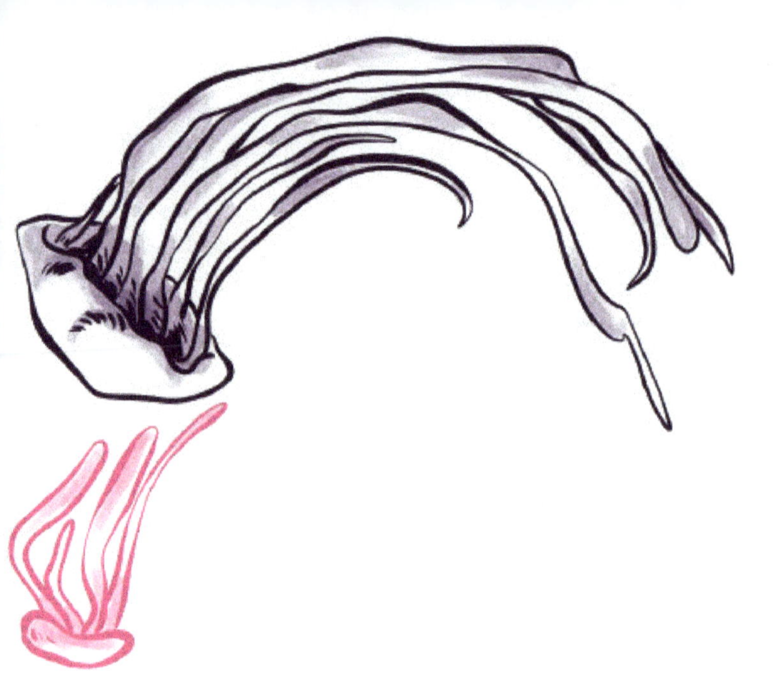

THE JELLYFISH

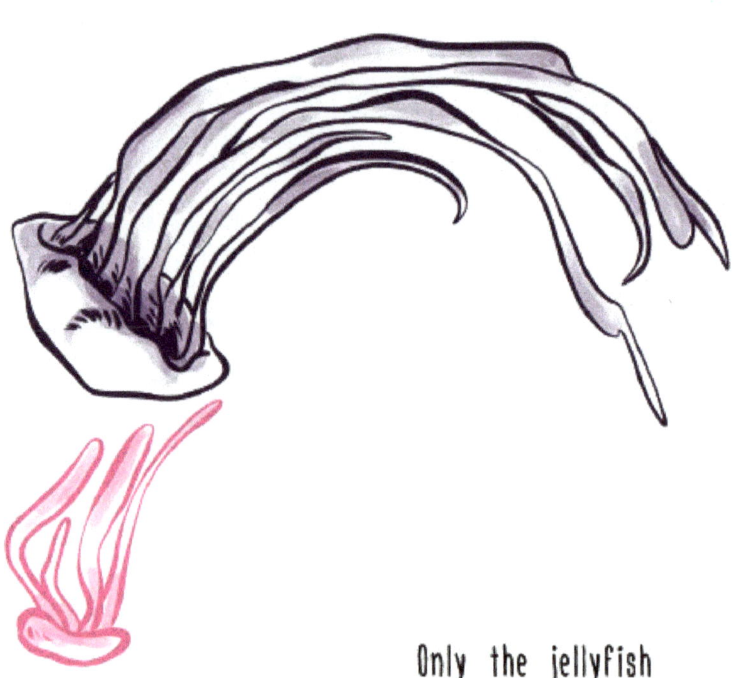

Only the jellyfish
Can live without a mind
Drifting through the sea
Beauty that dazzles mankind

I watch
And crave
Their lifestyle
So carefree

Jellyfish
Thoughts that don't exist
A body so fluid
Untouchable by predators

If I could just become the jellyfish
If I could just live in a world
Where I am in need of nothing
And nothing is in need of me
No mind and no heart

No more pressure
No more stress
No more thoughts

If I could just become the jellyfish

FINE

Fine
I'm fine
So fine
So fantastically
Fine

At least that's what I say
That's what
What I think
That's how
How I act

But deep down
So deep
My mind can't reach

Where my soul is weak
Where I am vulnerable

And you know this
Because of how deep
How deep you must go

I'm fine
So fine
Feeling
Incredible
Nothing
Everything

All is fine

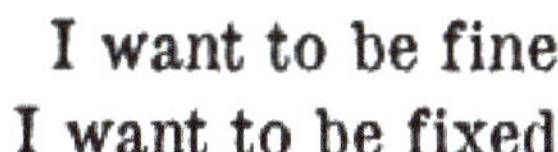

I want to be fine
I want to be fixed

I want to be whole
With happiness and joy
I want to

Be real
No more masking
No more covering up

All the negative feelings
All the uncomfortable feelings

Feelings that linger
Feelings that bring tears
Feelings that bring fears
Feelings I don't want

Feelings that deserve to be seen
Feelings that deserve to be felt
Feelings that deserve to heal

But they only can
When I stop hiding

Hiding from THESE feelings
I'm fine

I'm really really not
Fine

I'M NOT A
RETARD

"Retard" they all say and laugh
I don't find it very funny
I wish they would stop on my behalf
It makes me feel quite like a dummy

"It's just a joke," they all respond
This makes it hard to speak
I try to act nonchalant
I've heard them call me a freak

They tell me that they're my friends
Do they think that makes it all better?
Now I've been thinking of ways to make it all end
Terror strikes over me whenever we are together

I try to pretend that I don't care
But when that word is mentioned
All logic disappears
So that's how I got a suspension

"Retard" a boy says to me
This time I didn't take it as well
Next thing I knew, he wasn't smiling with glee
Now I'm sure I'll go to hell

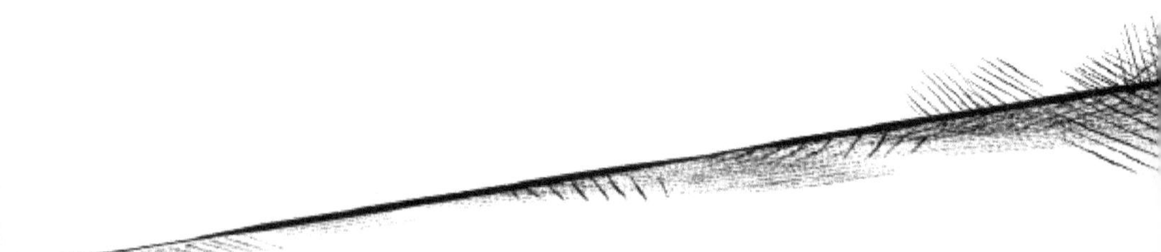

Why did my life have to be this way
I told everyone I wasn't stupid
My parents glared at me that day
They called me a doofus

For my words could not explain my actions
Alone at the house for days
My so-called friends had the same reactions
None of it was praise

People should think about their words
Maybe if people cared
They would realize it felt like stabbing swords
At least next time, I'll be prepared

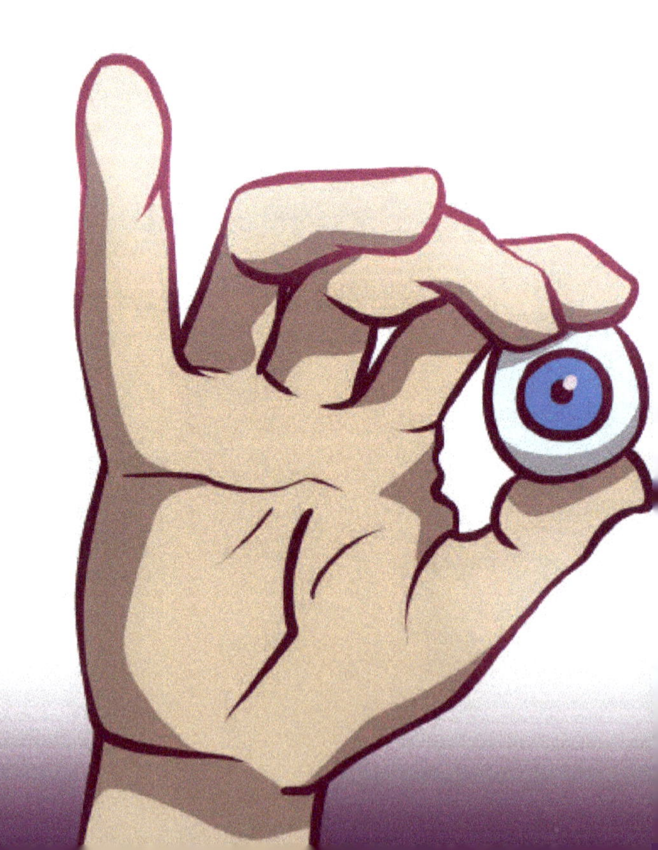

LOOK
AT
ME

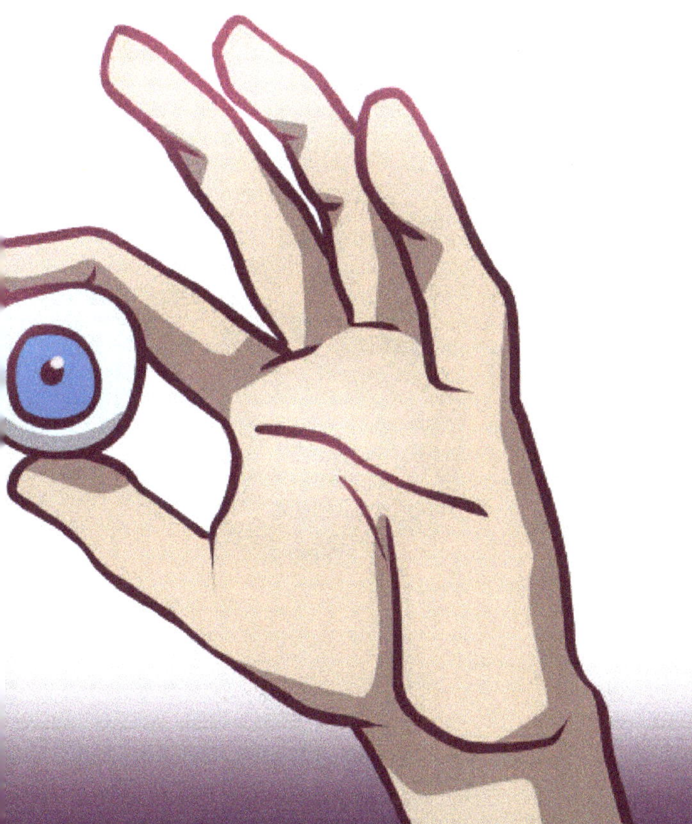

No one is willing
Willing to understand

I've tried to ask for help
I don't like your reactions

Your doubt
Your scrutiny
Your anger at my pain

Your solutions are silly and stupid
Drinking lots of water
Cleaning my depression room
Or just thinking happy thoughts
Are Useless!

Will you look AT ME

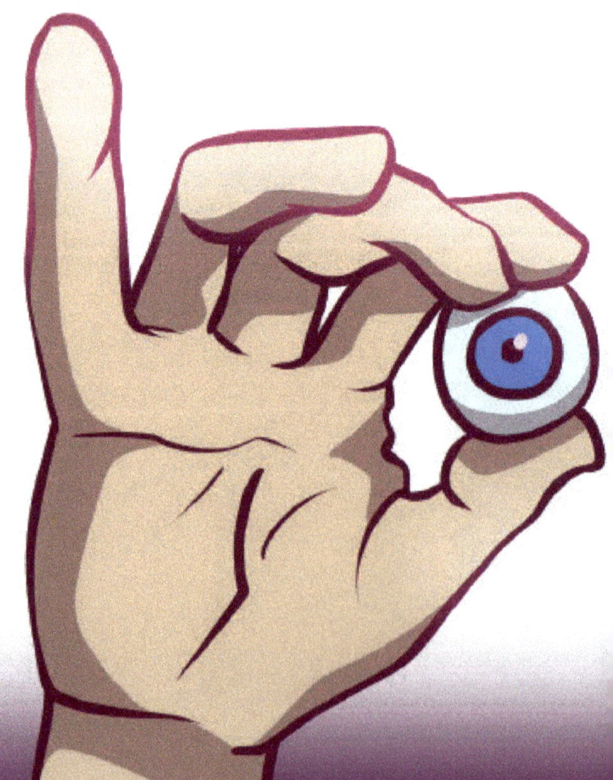

See beyond who you think I am
See beyond who you want me to be

I've tried all my options
I am doing everything
I can do to survive

I swear if you look at me with pity
I'm going to kill myself
I swear if you look at me with disappointment
I'm going to kill myself
I swear if you look at me and do not believe me
I'm going to kill myself

I want to kill myself

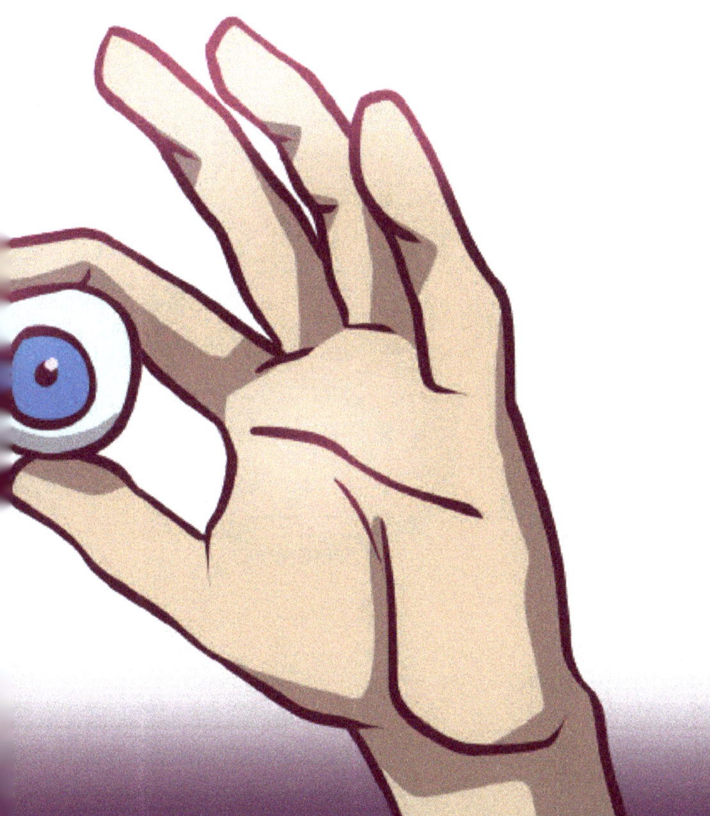

LOOK
AT
ME
The real version of me

I'm struggling to stay alive
What's the easiest way to die

Pay attention
My time is limited

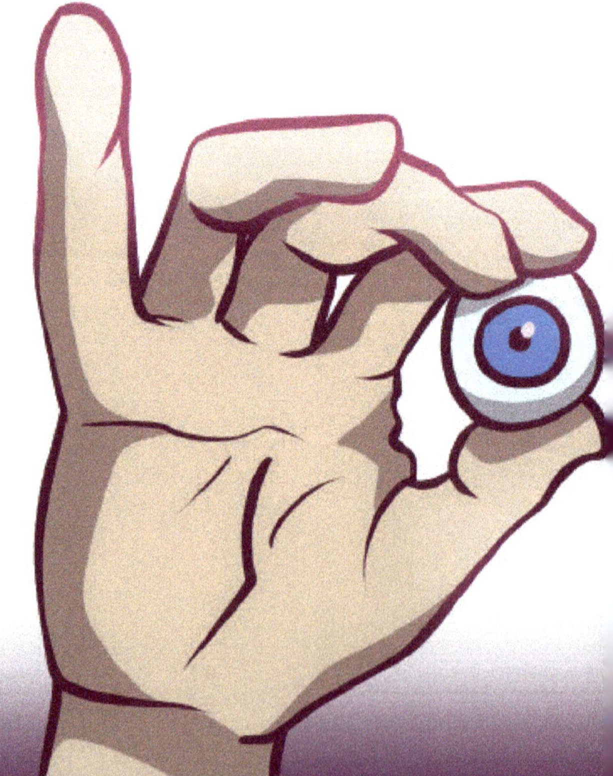

Look at me
Before it's too late
Before you don't get another chance
Before the last time
You see me
I'm lying in my casket
Ready to never be seen again

Open your eyes
And just
Look at me

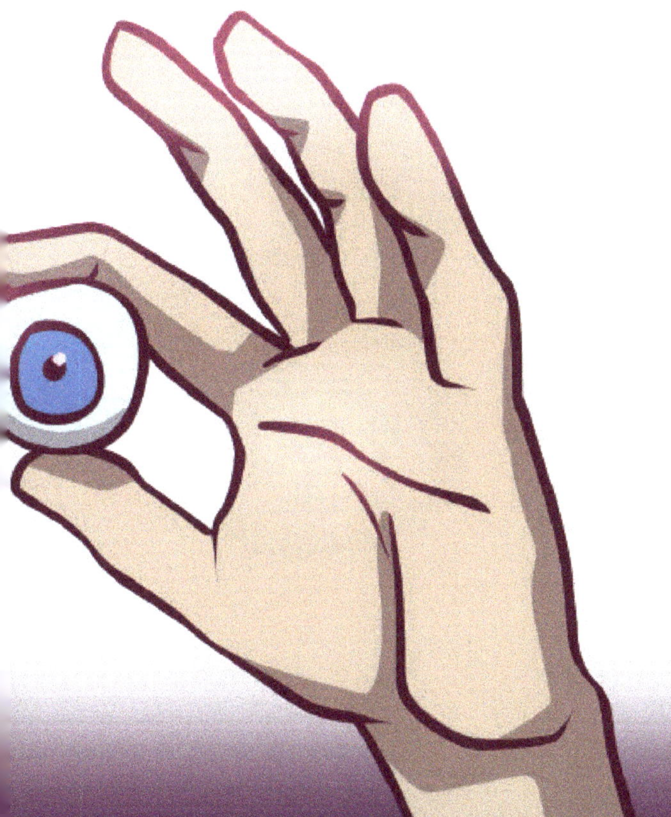

I want you to see me
Not who you think I am
Not who you wish I were

I fear you are blind
I fear
You won't ever see me
I fear
You won't even try

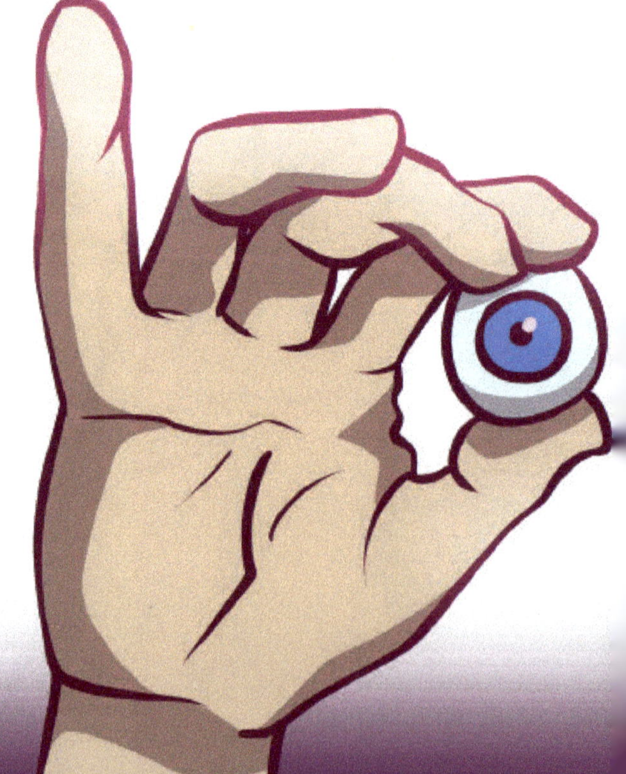

I get it
You are afraid
Just like I am
But please
Look at me
Just look at me

All I wish is to be seen

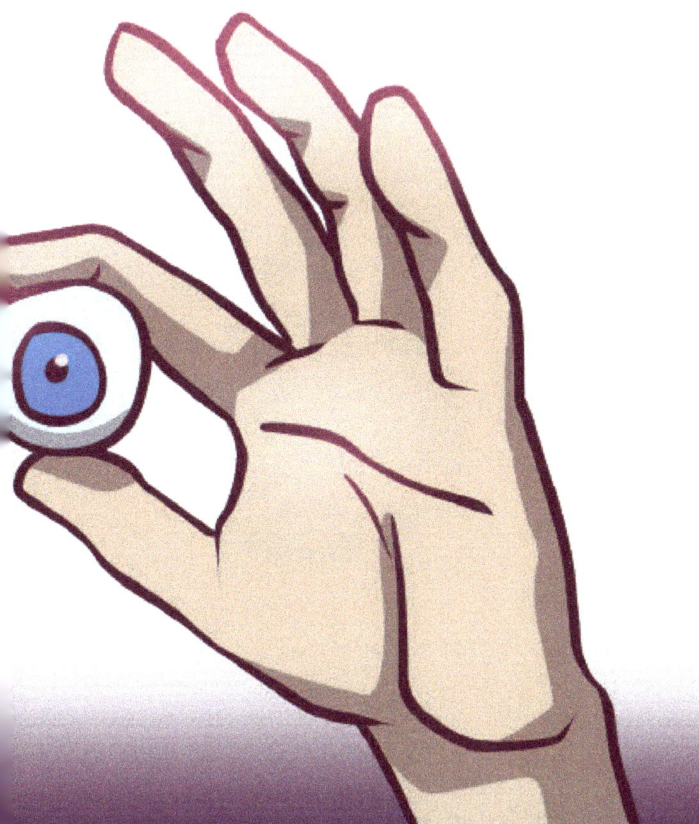

ILLOGICAL
LOGICAL

THOUGHTS

Make it stop
Please just make all these illogical
logical thoughts
Pull to
A halt.

I'm sick of fighting
And I'm sick trying
Make it all stop

My brain has betrayed me
I'm not in control
These thoughts come about
Dumping my sanity out
They dig a deep hole
And stuff me inside

Now I got nothing
So these illogical logical thoughts
enter my mind

I've got nothing but time to waste
Nothing but moments to spare
Memories of nothingness
That are making me despair

Make it all stop
I'm crying
I'm dying
I'm lying
I'm finding
There's no hope
No hope for me
I want to click my red shoes
Say one, two and three
And go home
Home to a place where things are
simple
Black and white
No gray
No middle
I don't know what I want
But I know this is NOT
what I need

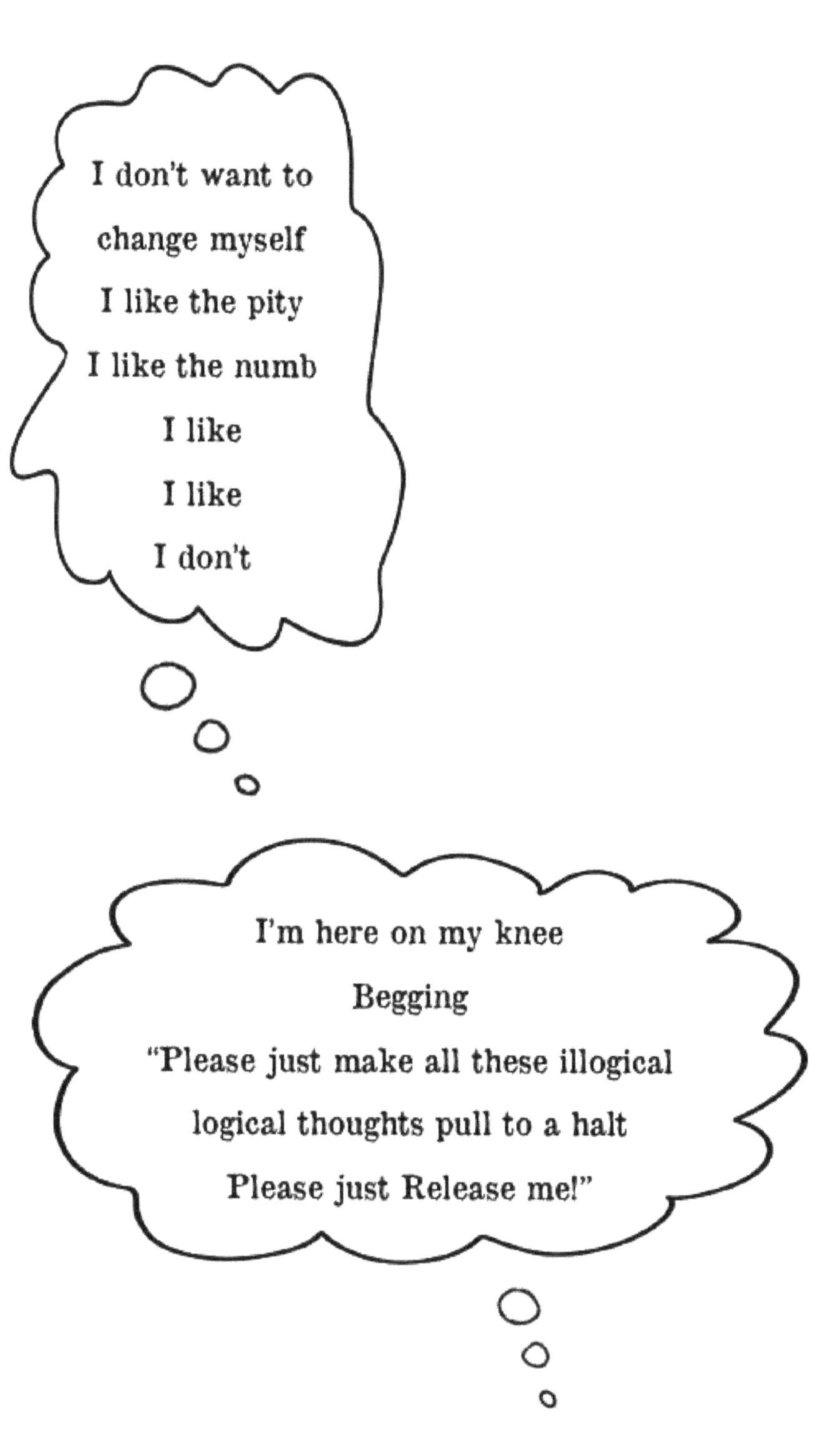

I don't want to change myself
I like the pity
I like the numb
I like
I like
I don't

I'm here on my knee
Begging
"Please just make all these illogical
logical thoughts pull to a halt
Please just Release me!"

Mentally
Ill

I am sick
Mentally ill
I have thoughts that drive me insane

They are logical and persuasive
Mean and abrasive
They argue
They bicker and fight
It's so damn loud in my head
Nothing can defeat them

Everyone around me is either winning or losing
Meanwhile, living is amusing
Life is just one big joke
And I'm not laughing

Life is a game

And I'm ready to end it

I didn't sign up to play

And I don't think I can handle another day

I have

Nothing left to gamble

Just broken mess

Shattered

In pieces

For all to see

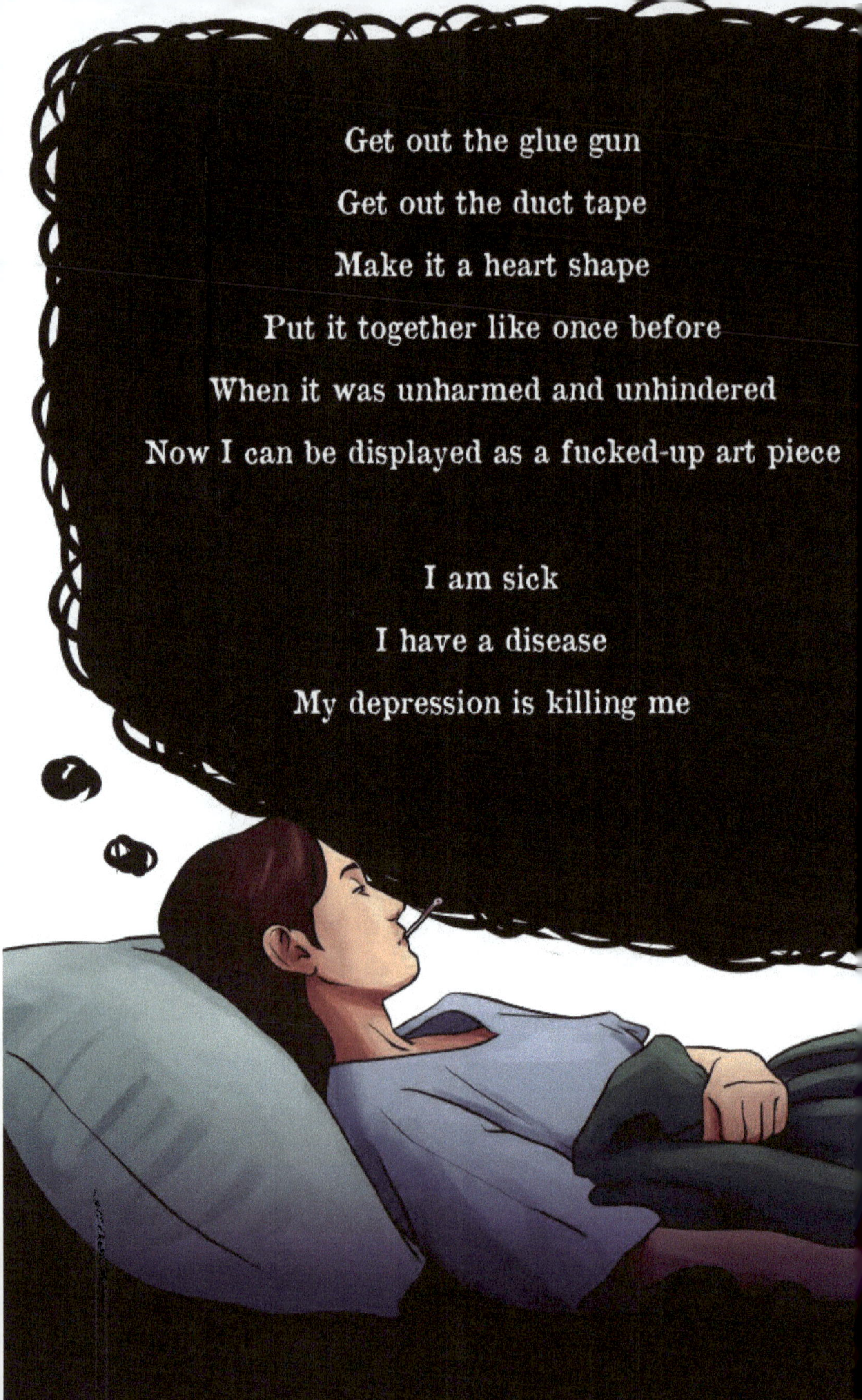

Get out the glue gun
Get out the duct tape
Make it a heart shape
Put it together like once before
When it was unharmed and unhindered
Now I can be displayed as a fucked-up art piece

I am sick
I have a disease
My depression is killing me

I can see no end to this fight

struggling

crying

And then I let myself have

One final goodbye

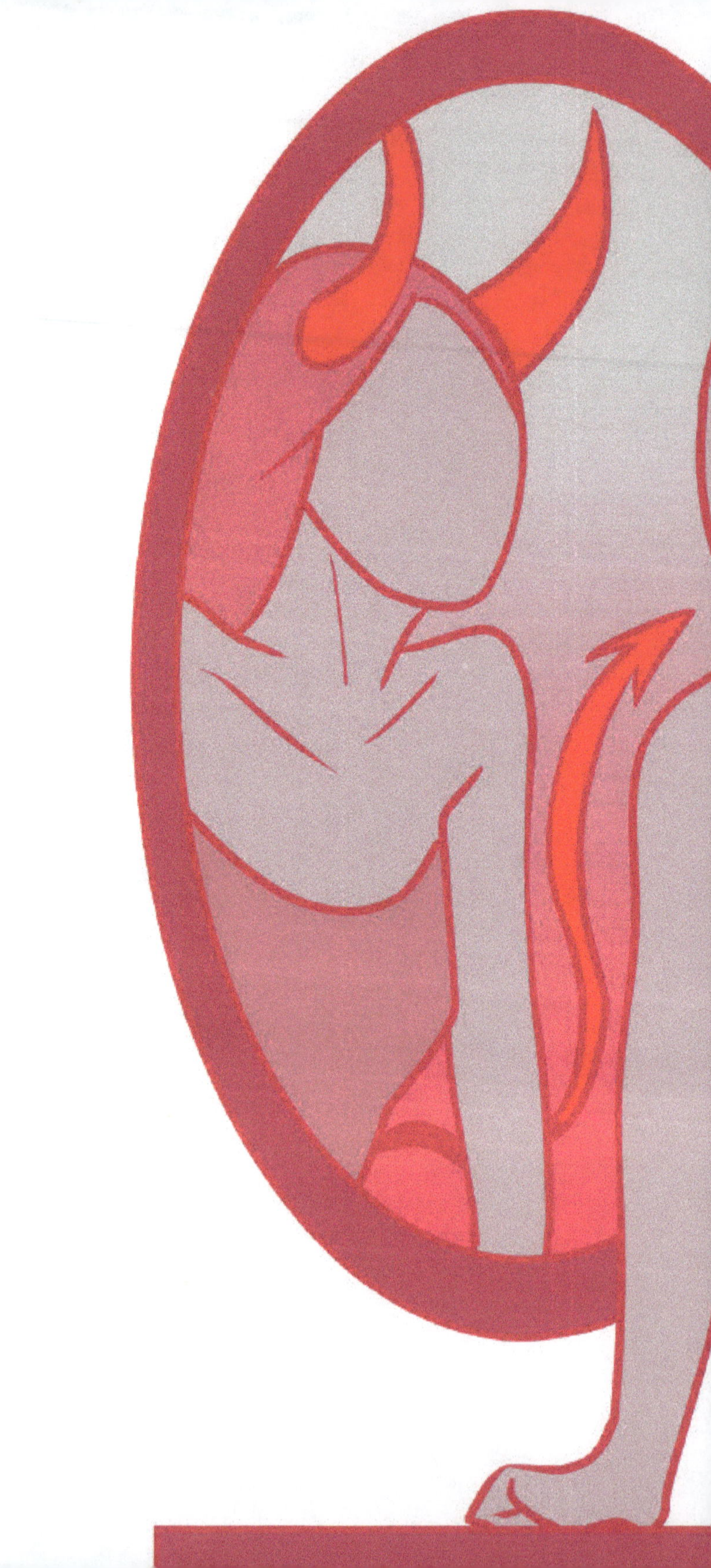

Am I
a
Bad
Person

Am I a bad person?
Do I deserve to live?

I wonder what I'm worth
How valuable my life is

Am I a bad person?
If I am not useful
If I am not helpful
If I do not make a
   significant amount of
   change in the world
Am I then a bad person?

I don't want to be a
   bad person
So I try to be useful
I try to be helpful
I try to make a significant
   amount of change in the world

Is that selfish?
Does that make me a bad person

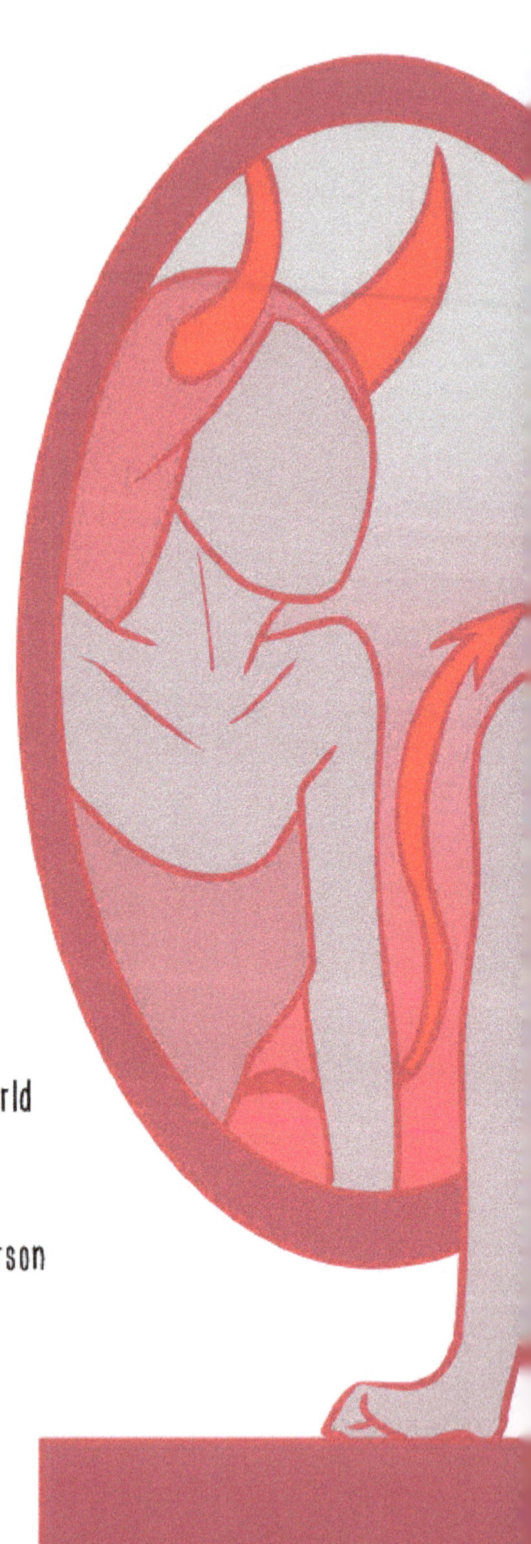

I give everything to everyone
Every part of me is not mine to own
But rather mine to donate

People come to me for help
But my shop is not open.
I have nothing left to give.
Everything is spoiled.
Everything is rotten.
My happiness has been corrupted.
I no longer can give

Does that make me a bad person?

Failing to serve. Failing to try.
I've given so much
Nothing left to give
Time to give up

Is that a bad thing?
Am I a bad person?

Was I helping myself or them?
Do I feed off their need for me?

Am I a bad person?
Do I do bad deeds?

I am now useless
And
No one wastes their time on
  a damaged product

Person to thing, thing to
  useful, useful to broken,
  broken to dust

Nothing left
But a bad person.
A bad useless thing

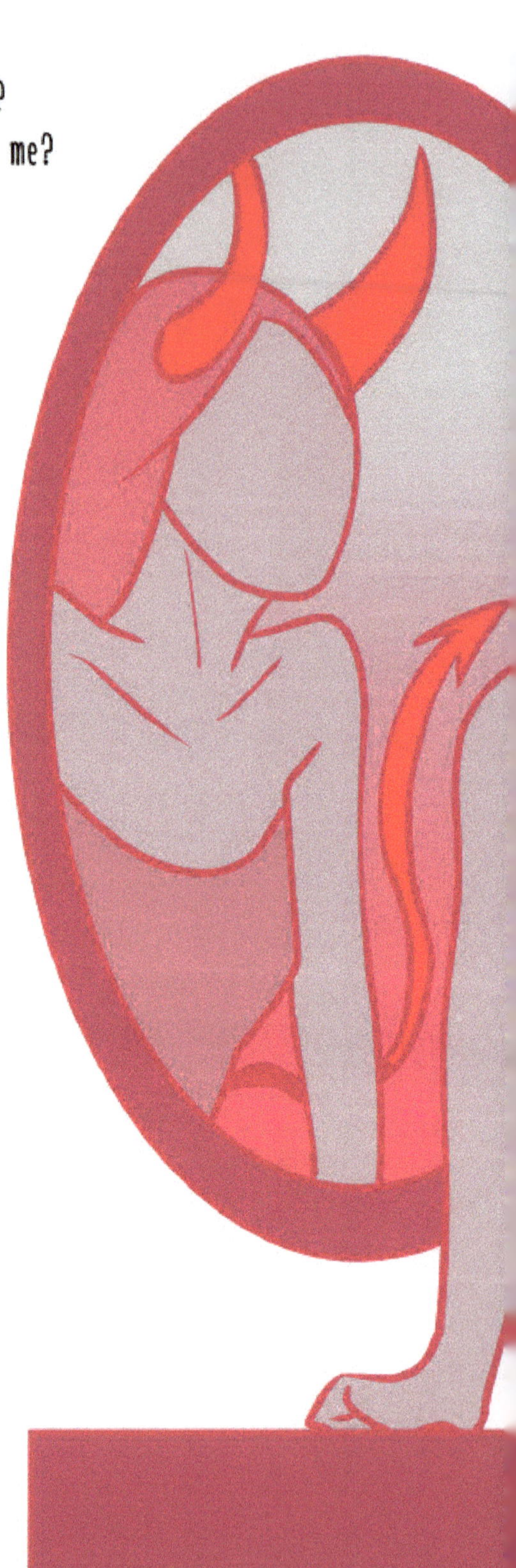

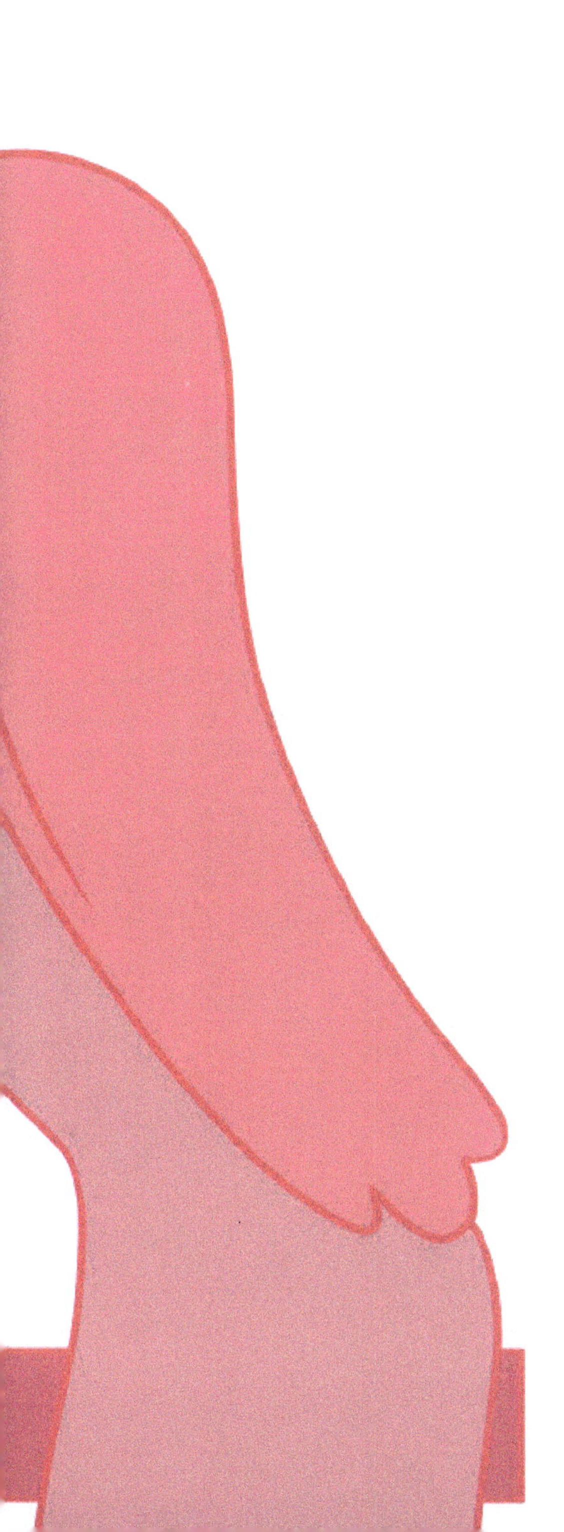

Living

or

Dying

Depression is a demon. It holds you. Holds
your hand. Climbing deeper and deeper into
your mind. Crawling its way into your heart.
Consuming your being. Causing you to believe
that you are one. Now you are powerless. Well
at least that's what it wants you to believe.
You believe it. Finding yourself, drowning in
your thoughts. Attached to your bed. Unwilling
to do the simplest things in your life. Moving
is a chore - Labeled laziness. Living is an
option - Called craziness.

Depression is a demon. Unseen. Unwanted.
Unpreventable.

This demon has a mind of its own. Speaking to you at all times. Times when you are joyful. Times when you are low. Times when all you want, all you beg for is sleep. Sleep is just another trick in the bag that depression has control over. Whether you sleep, whether you don't, depression is in the driver's seat.

Sleeping is an escape, an opportunity. Some can sleep peacefully. Whisked away by their fantasies. Unable to cope with the things that happen when they're awake.

Sleeping can be a struggle. A prize never earned. Hour upon hours of tossing and turning. Terrors of the imagination haunt those who are "gifted" the chance to actually

fall

asleep!

And yet there are those up 'til sunrise. Insomnia cuddling their tired bodies. Continuing to shove unwanted thoughts into their restless minds.

You would hope with all these plagues, it would just end there.
That's when you would be mistaken.

Like any abusive lover. It takes, and takes, and gives so you stay.

You begin to like the loneliness that envelops your day. Craving the times when everyone's away.

Like any abusive lover. It becomes your only friend. Your only companion. Separated from family and loved ones. Depression is your everything.

Once you are this far gone. You are helpless.
You are nothing without your depression.

You can't leave.

All happiness, forgotten.
All hope, lost.
All beauty, disturbed.

Depression's claws clutch your world.
Craving its name.
Engraved in the stone.
Bold letters. As bold as its narcissistic
personality.

You are the slave. It is the master.

Chains around your throat.
Piercing the skin ever so slight. But if you
move without permission, then it digs without
mercy.

No compassion, when you're bleeding. No
compassion when you're shrieking. No
compassion when you're dying.

Dying, not such a scary word when you're
filled to the brim with emptiness.

Dying. Others die all the time. Some are
missed. All are forgotten. They become stories,
like they never even existed.

Would people miss you?

This is the first question that means
depression is winning.

Is there a point to resume living?

This is the second. Your downfall is soon.
When you reach the third. No one else can
reach you.

Depression can now silence the voices that try
to help. They are no match. This is your battle.
You have been stabbed. You have now fallen.
You are in utter darkness.

You are afraid. As you plan your next actions.
Actions that now literally mean life or death.

When, how, and where?

To most, these words are not significant. Just
words. That hold no meaning. Words to an
investigation. Please investigate!

When
Will you die?

How
Will you do it?

Where
Will your final moments be?

This is the true meaning of suicide.

SHUT UP BIRDS

"Be brave" they say
Like a squawking bird
High above the ground
They watch safe
Safe

As I the prey
Is devoured

Devoured by fear
Depression
Anxiety
Devoured by uncertainty
Devoured entirely

"Be brave" they mock
Know the harm is mine
All mine
And mine alone

They don't understand
I don't want to
I don't have to

My decision
My choice
My life

"Be brave" they on repeat
Watching, Watching, Watching
From high above
All they do is
WATCH
All I do is DO

But it's not enough
Never enough

Those greedy, greedy birds

What do they expect of me
These words of little use
Be brave
Be strong
The fucking nonsense of it all

I want to give in
I want to give up
What right do those birds have
When they can fly

They have no right
To give advice
To dare pretend
They don't know what it's like
To be tethered to the ground

Those stupid birds
Shut up
And leave me alone

Broken House

90 PERCENT OF ME IS BROKEN

A HOUSE BEYOND REPAIR

THE CEILING IS CRACKING
THE FLOORS ARE ATTACKING

WOOD BOARDS SPRUNG UPWARDS
TO TRAP YOU AS IT BREAKS APART

WHEN WILL YOU REALIZE
IT'S TIME TO LEAVE

STOP USING YOUR STUPID EMOTIONS

USE YOUR BRAIN
YOUR LOGIC
YOUR KNOWLEDGE

I AM CAUSING YOU PAIN

THIS HOUSE WILL ONLY BRING MISERY.
PLEASE GET OUT WHILE YOU CAN
YOU MUST BE AWARE.
IT CREAKS
CRUMBLES
CRASHES
DISINTEGRATES BEFORE YOUR VERY EYES

I BEG YOU. DO NOT ALLOW IT TO TAKE YOU DOWN

THE WORK FOR REPAIR
WILL TAKE TIME
WILL TAKE MONEY

ALL THINGS THAT SHOULD NOT BE WASTED ON A
HOUSE THAT NEEDS TO BE DECIMATED

IT OFFERS LITTLE
NEED MUCH MORE THAN SOME SCRIBBLES
PLANS ON A PAPER
NEVER MEANT FOR MUCH MORE

LEAVE ME
GET TO WHERE YOU ARE SAFE
FREE FROM THE BURDENS OF THIS HOUSE
THAT CAN BARELY PERFORM ITS MOST
IMPORTANT, ESSENTIAL USES

DON'T GET INVOLVED
IT'S NOT WORTH YOUR TIME
10 PERCENT OF ME IS FINE
BUT IT'S NOT ENOUGH

A CURSE
COVERED IN GRIME
MOLD
AND ROT

PLEASE CHOOSE
A HOUSE WHO IS 90 PERCENT FINE
10 PERCENT PROBLEMS
GIVES MORE THAN IT TAKES
LEAVES LESS THAT IT WAS LEFT

FOR I AM A HOUSE BEYOND REPAIR

Perfect

Perfect

The hateful way it sits in my mouth
Perfect

The little lies I spread
Perfect

Every day
perfect

Everyone
Perfect

Family life
Perfect

Grades
Perfect

I'm
Perfect

Always
Perfect

The way I invalidate myself
Perfect

The ways I keep the thoughts at bay
Perfect

Unwilling to admit anything else but
Perfect

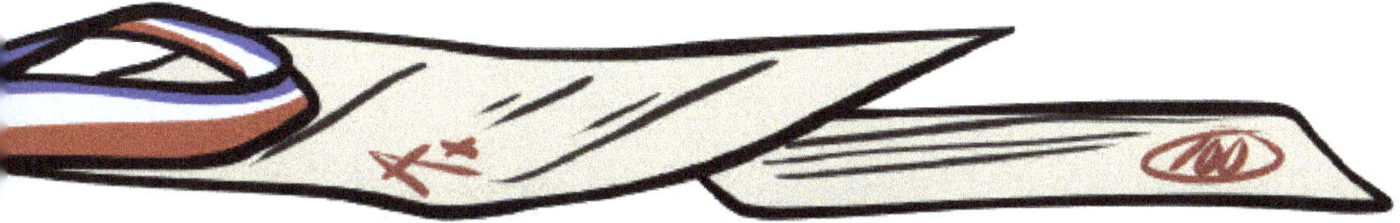

Every day isn't perfect
My life isn't perfect
I want to be perfect
But I'm not

Damaged
Defective
Faulty
Flawed
Imperfect
Broken
And human

HAPPY THOUGHTS

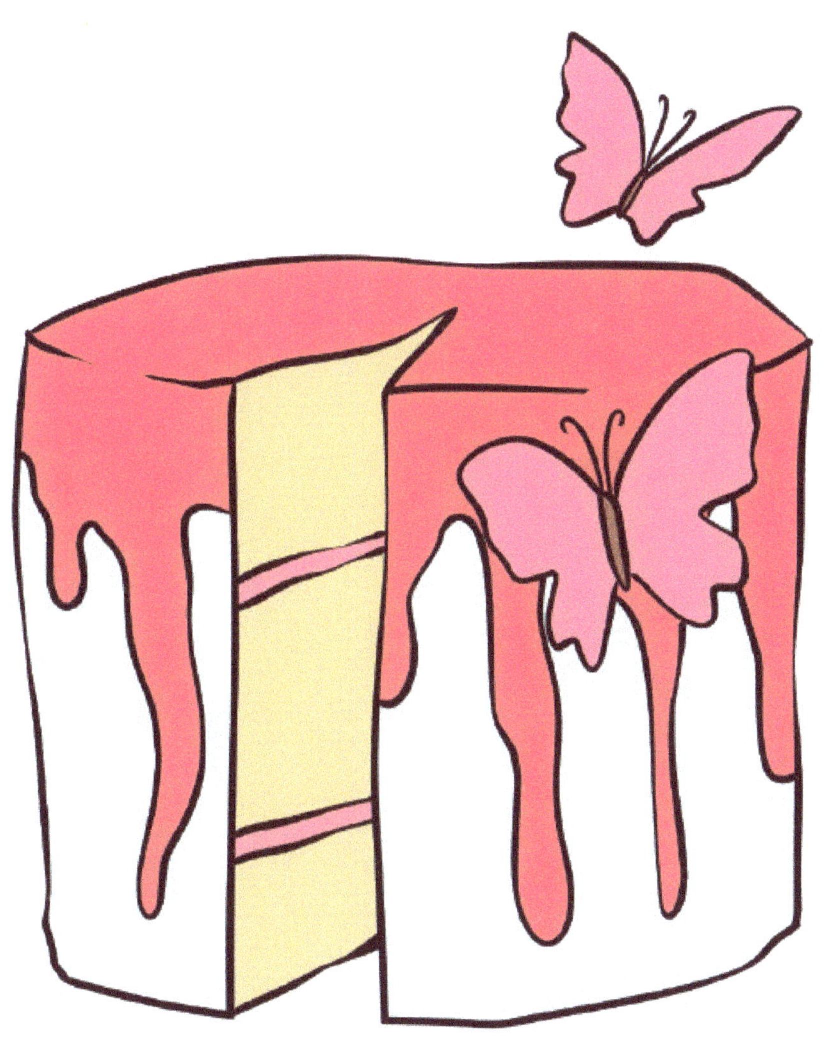

                    Butterflies
                     Dancing
              Fluttering around a cake
                   My happy place

                    Happy thoughts
                    Happy thoughts

        Happy thoughts begin to fall apart
                  I must keep thinking

                       Happ
                                    y

                       Hap
                                 p
                                          y
                       Ha
                                p
                                       p
                                              y

Happy thoughts fall apart
Happy thoughts break
Into a million parts
No way to go back to those happy thoughts
Scattered and splattered
I'll never
Have happy thoughts
Ever again

Why did my happy thoughts leave?
Why have they abandoned me?

Happy thoughts have
Died
Now only ghostly figures of their
previous self.

Oh, my budding flower
Happiness isn't
Something
That you can will to happen

Just because you allow yourself to feel
Jealousy
Anger
Sadness
Grief

That doesn't mean you won't feel happiness again

All emotions are powerful enough
To change the world
Change society
Change minds
Heal Hearts

Don't fear your negative emotions
Don't shove them down
Down
Down
Til they erupt unexpectedly

Instead
Value them
Express them
Learn
Love
So you can really
LIVE

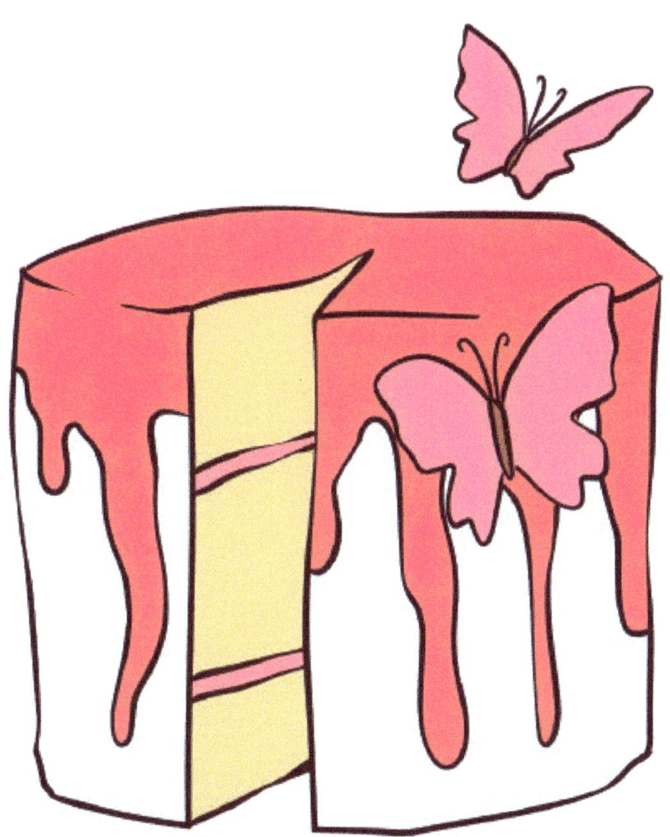

DRIP
DROP

Drip drop
Rain

Drippy drop
Nothing but pain

Drippy drop
Nothing but fear

Drip drop
Nothing left but the thundering
In my mind

Drippy drop
Crying
Drippy drop
Screaming

Drip drop
I'm drowning, I said
Drippy drop
I'm dying, you dickhead

It's all coming to an end
Drip drop
Drippy drop
Drop dead

STOP

Open your eyes
Look around
Reach out your hand
And breath

Give yourself a chance
To weather the storm

I promise
You're worth it
Don't give up
I know

You are drowning
But you can stand up
And the drowning
The drowning is
Only three feet deep

Drip drop
Drippy drop
Just live

VOICES

I'm scared
I'm alone
I'm on one thread
One thread to falling apart
Do you think I'm ok?
Think with your heart

Trying to silence
These sounds
These voices are so damn loud
These voices I'm hearing
As my head pounds

I'm so scared
I'm so alone
Why do you think I'm ok?

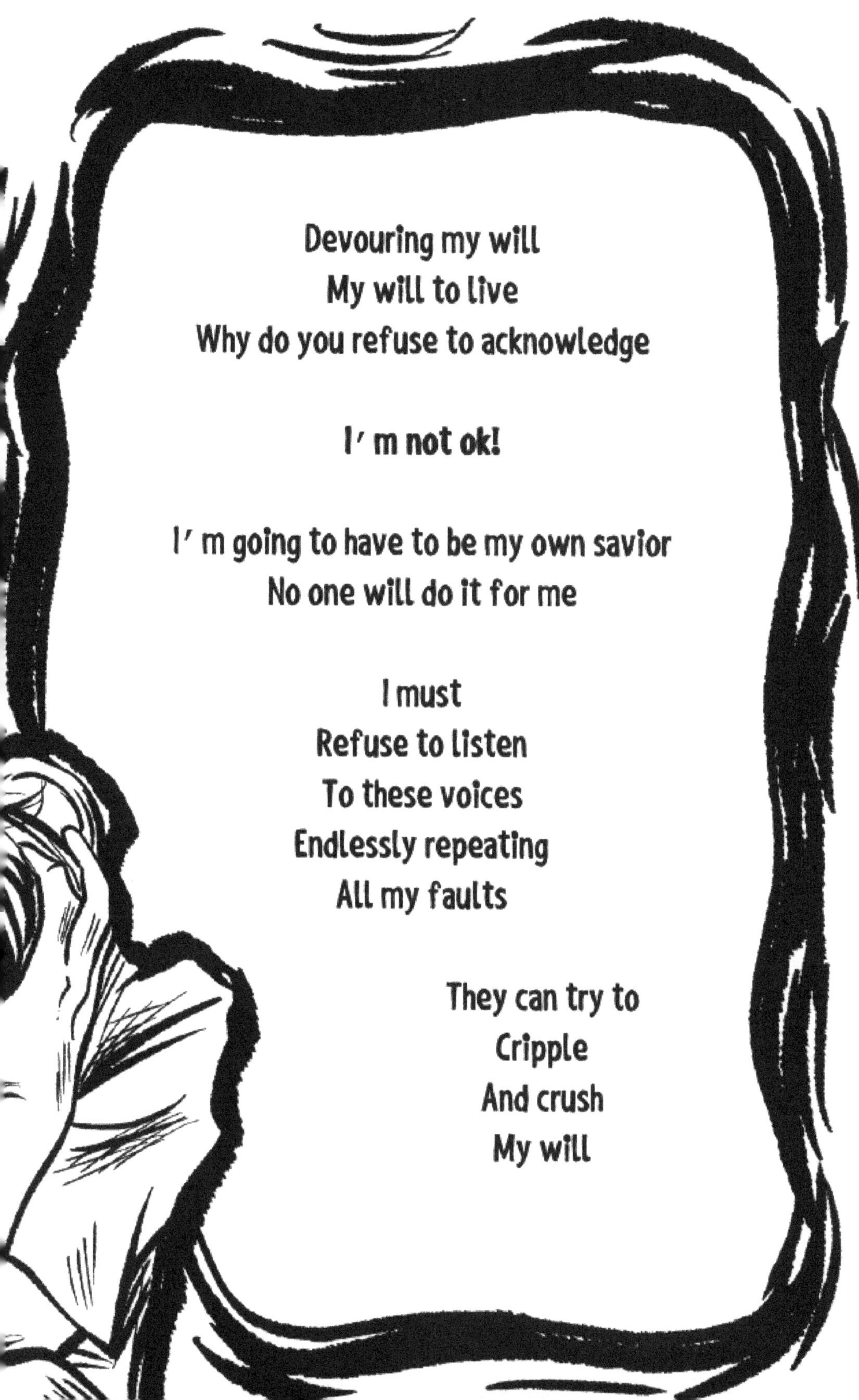

Devouring my will
My will to live
Why do you refuse to acknowledge

I' m not ok!

I' m going to have to be my own savior
No one will do it for me

I must
Refuse to listen
To these voices
Endlessly repeating
All my faults

They can try to
Cripple
And crush
My will

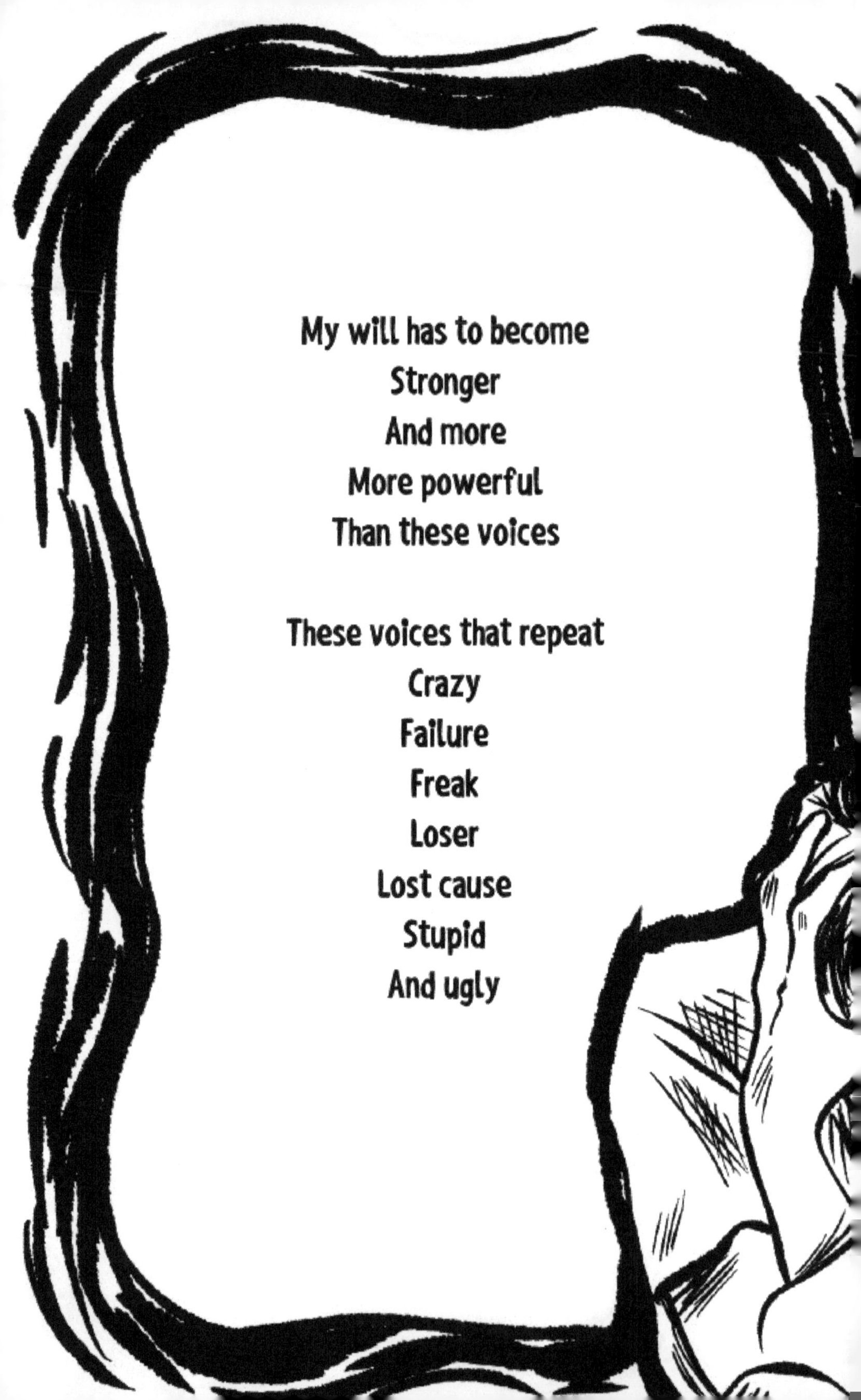

My will has to become
Stronger
And more
More powerful
Than these voices

These voices that repeat
Crazy
Failure
Freak
Loser
Lost cause
Stupid
And ugly

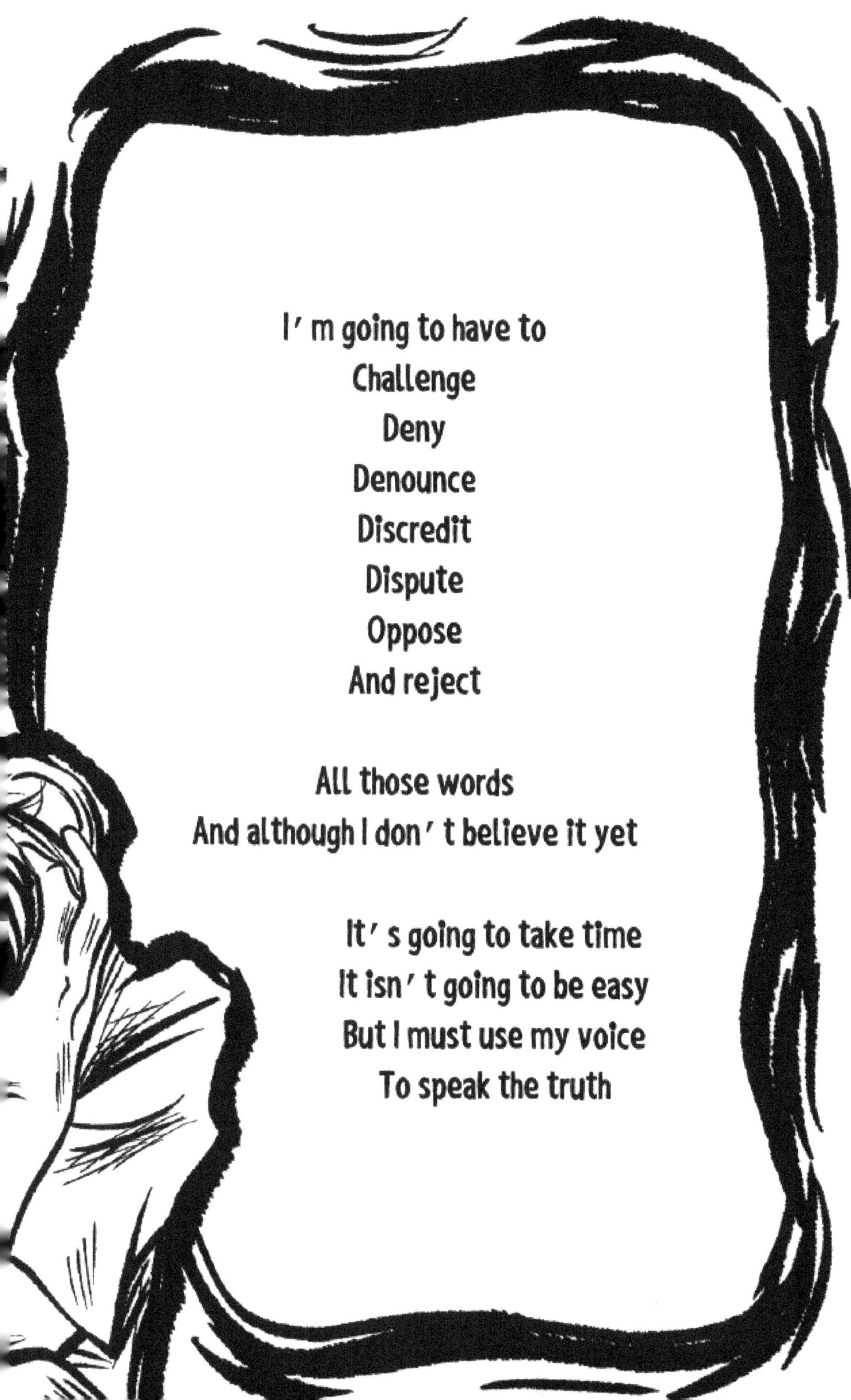

I'm going to have to
Challenge
Deny
Denounce
Discredit
Dispute
Oppose
And reject

All those words
And although I don't believe it yet

It's going to take time
It isn't going to be easy
But I must use my voice
To speak the truth

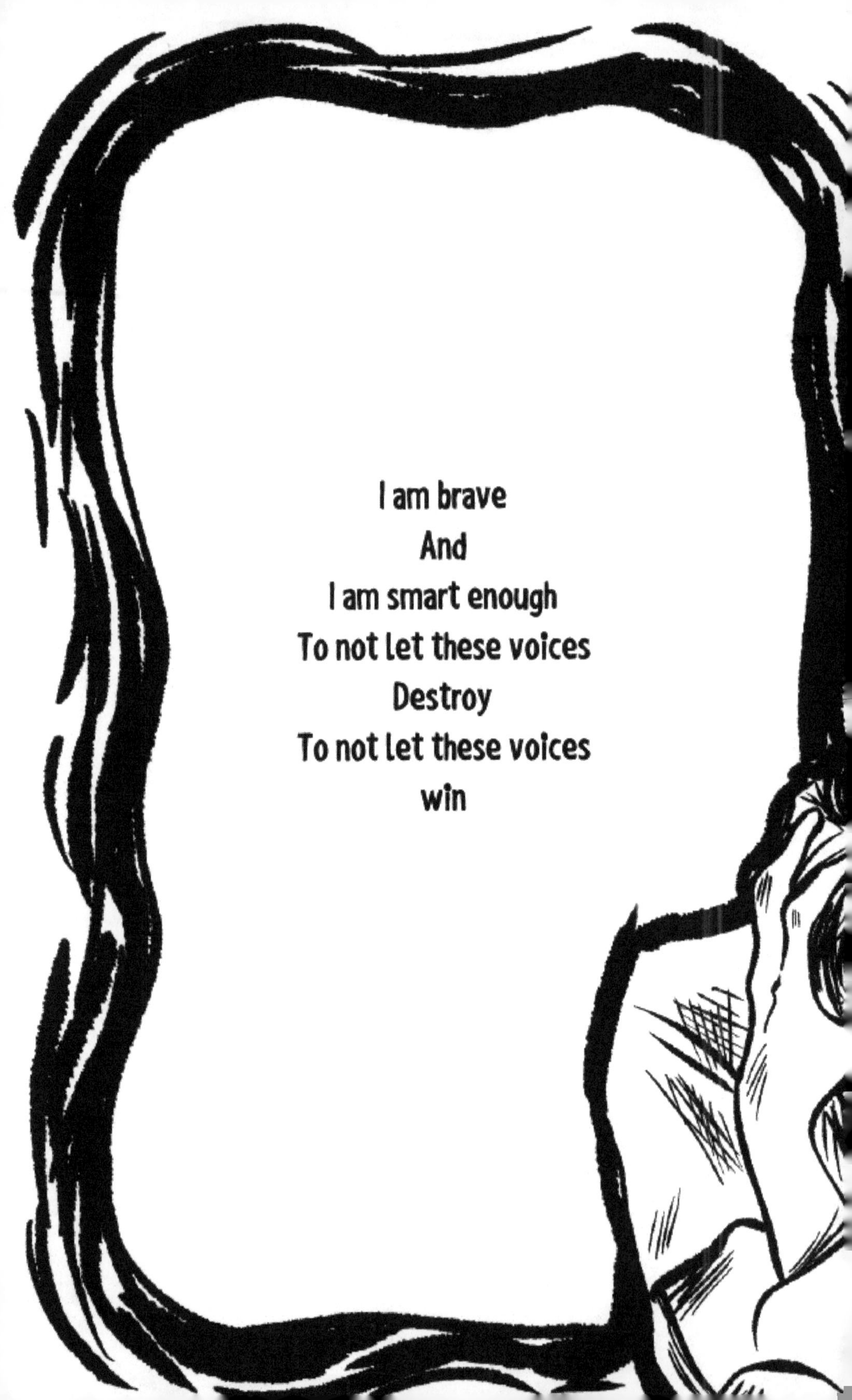
I am brave
And
I am smart enough
To not let these voices
Destroy
To not let these voices
win

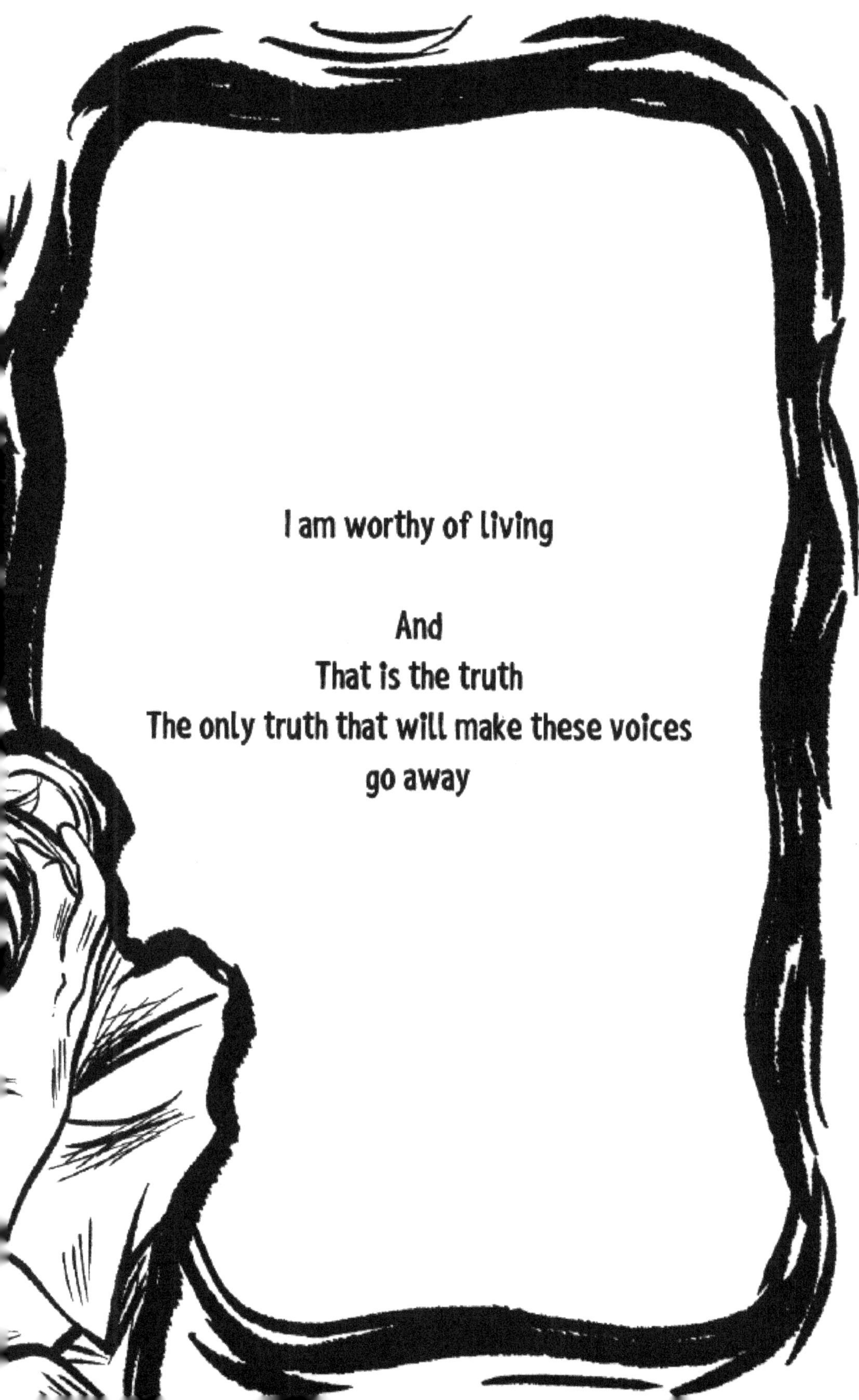

I am worthy of living

And
That is the truth
The only truth that will make these voices
go away

WHY
DO I
MATTER

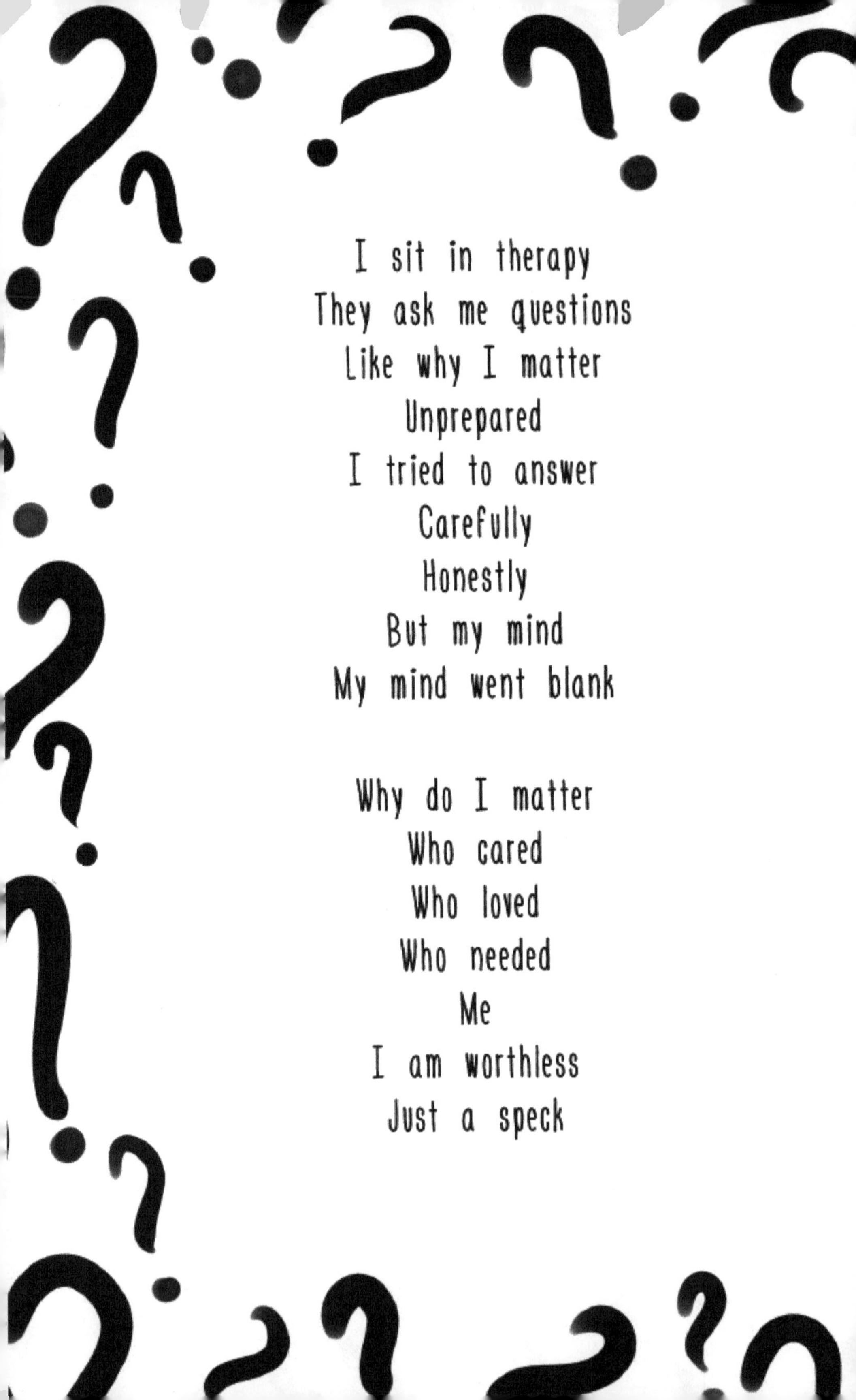

I sit in therapy
They ask me questions
Like why I matter
Unprepared
I tried to answer
Carefully
Honestly
But my mind
My mind went blank

Why do I matter
Who cared
Who loved
Who needed
Me
I am worthless
Just a speck

Why did I matter?
My brain repeated
Over
And over
Why did I matter?

Why
Did
I
Matter

Of all people
Of all living beings

Why did I matter
The question pleaded
To be answered
Yet I stood dumbfounded
Why did I matter?

I matter because...

Again, the question stopped me
Shook me
Begging
Why do you matter?

Astounded
That I could not answer
Such a simple question
Such a basic
QUESTION

Instead, I asked
Why do I not matter?
Why do I think I'm worthless?
Why I am nothing?

And yet
THAT question was even
more complex

I stumbled through my thoughts
Did I matter because of an act of
God?
Did I matter simply because I existed?
Did I matter because I wasn't in my
casket?
Did I matter because my parents had
sex?

None of it felt right
Maybe
Just maybe
I matter because
I choose to matter
I matter to myself
And that's all that matters

LUCKY

I believe I am Lucky
Others believe I am Lucky

People tell me
"If you are Lucky
You must not complain
Otherwise, you are ungrateful."

Lucky
Lucky
Lucky

How dare I say
That I have troubles
That I have pain
How dare I say
That I have problems
That I have struggles

Everyone thinks
I'm just so ungrateful
Because I'm just so
Fucking Lucky

But, so are they

Living life isn't "easy" for anyone
Everyone experiences pain
Everyone is allowed to complain

I am grateful someone once told me
"Just because someone else is drowning ten feet
deep
And you are only drowning three
You both still need help
After All
You are both drowning
No matter how deep."

I am Lucky

THE
ONE
YOU
WANT

I try to be obedient
Passive and Docile

I try to be good
Worthy and kind

I try to be happy
Loved and bubbly

But nothing will please you

You command
Yell and insult

Everyone knew
Yet they did nothing

Then amazed at the cutting
Cutting at the threads

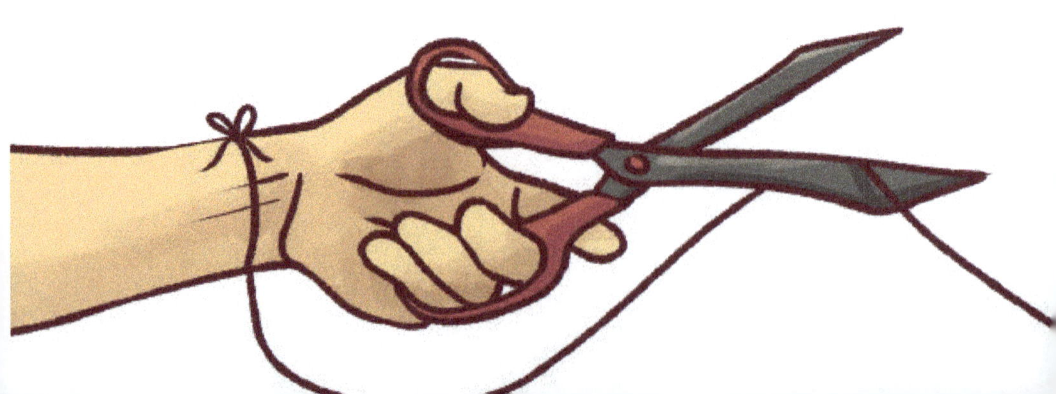

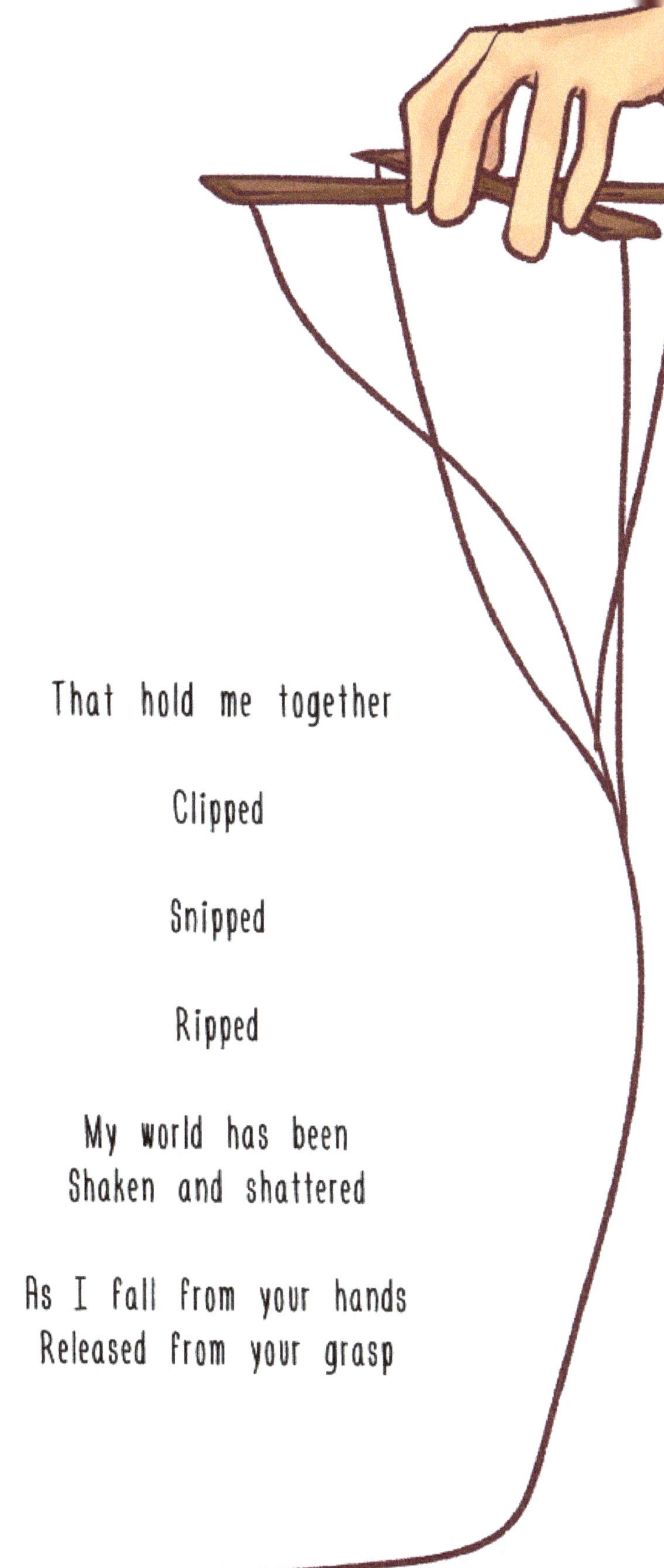

That hold me together

Clipped

Snipped

Ripped

My world has been
Shaken and shattered

As I fall from your hands
Released from your grasp

I am
No longer pulled forward
No longer pulled up

No longer is this just a
threat
I'm done being your marionette

At first
I thought I wouldn't be able
to get back up
I thought I needed you
Your Control

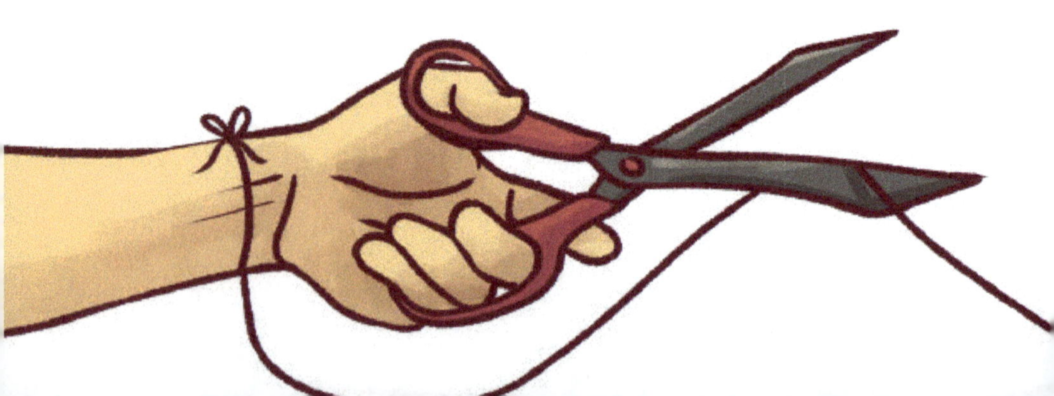

Your pull
Your force

But I am not your puppet
And I do not need any puppeteer

I am not as weak as you led me
To always believe

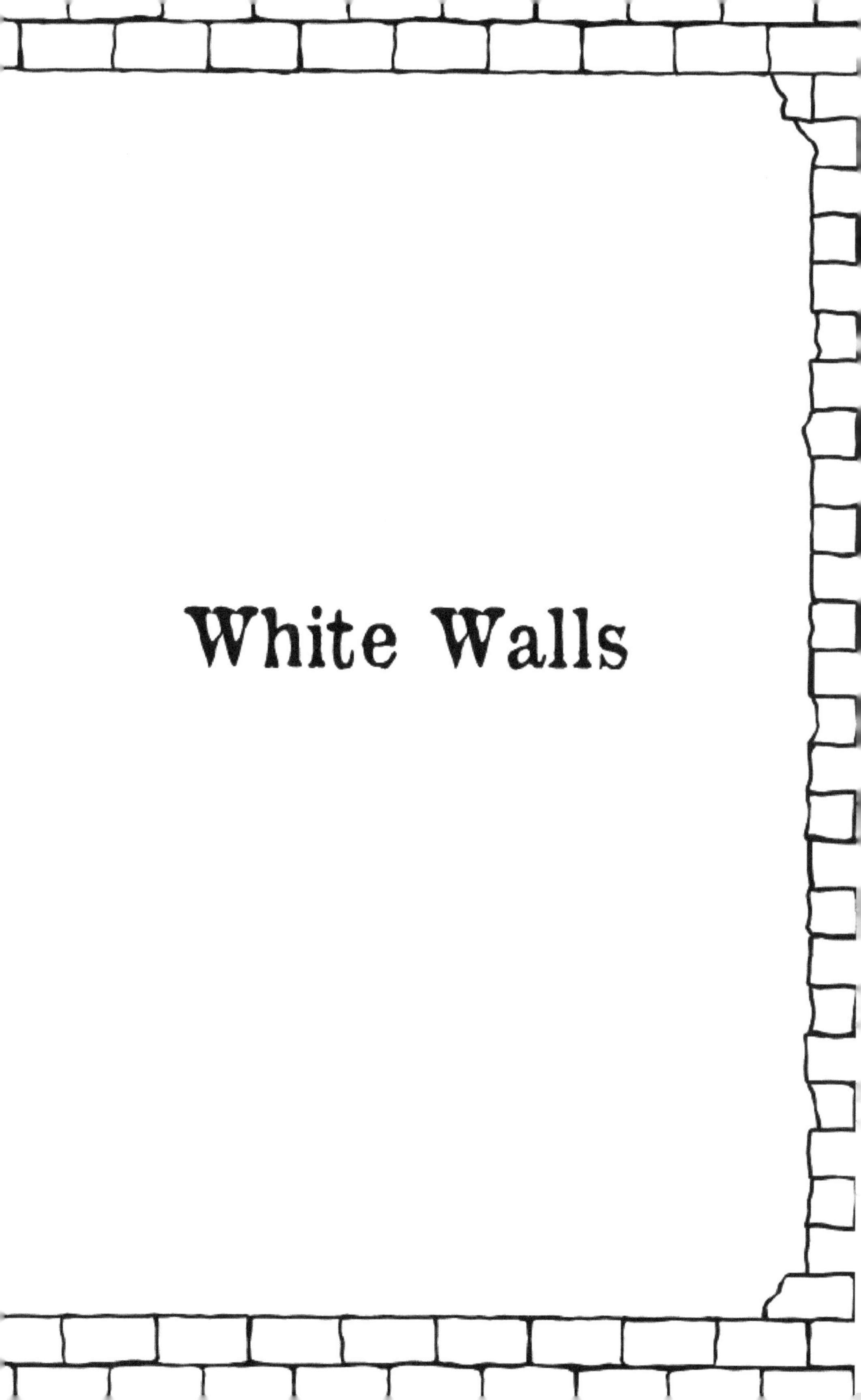

White Walls

My friend and I used to joke about the place where the walls are white, your clothes are white, and wherever you look, it is white. A place where you have plenty of company because you have the voices in your head and the demons that stalk you in the corners of the room. A place where you are never alone because there's a camera always watching you.

This place was supposed to only exist in our wildest imaginations. Mental illness was a sickness only for "other people." After all, we were normal, perfectly normal.Mental illness was something that would never, could never, affect us.

It had just turned dark on what should have been an ordinary Friday when my dad walked me into the ER. I wore a persona that showed no sign of pain. "Conceal, don't feel, don't let it show."

Another episode of the unreal. Another moment. Another nightmare. My life, nothing more than a figment of reality.

My bubbly demeanor quickly appeared. I gave them a performance. No signs of pain. No signs of illnesses.

I lit up a smile on my face. I turned on my giggles. I seemed like such a happy person.

"Just let me kill myself."

All the giggles and smiles in the world could not deflect from my horrifying words.

Now they send me away; I need to be fixed. It's simple, doctors in white coats can fix me.

Blue clothes, broken people, and bright white walls. I was here. I had officially entered the mental hospital, the nightmare of a place where I would stay for the next three days.

It's impossible to describe my thoughts that swirled and spun when I arrived. There are no words in this world that would be able to even explain the chaos of where I was trapped. My head was loud, my heart was loud, and the people were even louder.

That's when it happened.

The staff rounded up a few of the girls. One girl was crying hysterically. What could they possibly want from us? They announced that we were moving to a different ward.

"You four are good girls, so we're going to place you with other good girls."

They acted like we had won an award or something.

This was their first mistake. My first grudge.

"Good". The word struck as an insult. An underhanded way of presenting their biases. Since we were "good" they were going to move us, take us away from the new bonds we had formed, that kept us sane. I sat quietly. Twenty-four hours hadn't even passed, and already something felt blatantly wrong.

"Don't you understand," one of the girls pleaded, "I have to stay with my friend. I need her! Please don't take me away. Take someone else! Anyone else! Please." Another girl stood up pleading, "I'll go instead, just let her stay. Please!"

But their cries fell upon deaf ears. The staff was unconcerned with our feelings. It's ironic because we only got on this dark path of suicide, because we felt unheard, unwanted, and our feelings, misunderstood.

Without permission my legs stood up, my mouth began to argue. Over and over, I chastised the staff. I told them how they needed to ask our permission before they moved us. They needed to accept the answer no and show us some respect. However, they disregarded my words. The whole time they just scapegoated their actions as the doctor's orders.

"We have no control over this," the staff kept repeating in their high and mighty, overpowered, and apathetic tone.

Fragile, and already torn to pieces, myself and my companions tried our best to comfort one another. We despised our circumstances and this made us destroy every opportunity that was given to start anew.

Yet somehow, we grew. We grew together, holding each other close hoping and praying that we wouldn't be torn away from each other. Within hours we had become friends, siblings, daughters of common mistakes. For a small time period, we were happy, because we were together. We made up nicknames for each other. Babycakes, because she was thick. Lovebaby because she was flirtatious, Babygirl because she was sensitive,and lastly me, Frecklebaby because I had freckles.

I thought someone had died in the middle of the night. I woke up to hollering and tears running profusely down on Lovebaby.

"Bring her back! Don't lock her up! She's scared! Don't you care?" My roommate argued.

"What's going on?" I asked.

"They took her. Babygirl is locked up in that room. All alone in the darkness. She's...Scared. Frecklebaby do something, you're good with words."

Second mistake. Second grudge.

"Now Lovebaby, try to calm yourself, I'll handle this." I tried to ease my own panic. Now I was responsible for saving Babygirl. I couldn't bear to think how the others would treat me if I let them down. I went up to the charge nurse.

"Um, Miss, can you tell me what's happening?"

"This is none of your concern. Go back to your bedroom. Go back to sleep."

"I refuse to go back to sleep. She is my friend. I respectfully request to know what's happening to her. However, I will not allow you to walk all over me. I will not allow you to try to pacify me. We've already been unheard at this hospital, and I will not stand back as my friend is locked up without cause or reason." My voice stiffened with an authoritative command, "I will not leave until you tell me what has happened to Babygirl? Why is she being locked away in that dark room all alone?"

As if no one had ever stood their ground to this charge nurse before, the lady straightened-up in her chair. She looked down onto me in a most condescending way I presumed she knew how. She was provoking me and it was working. I held my breath, afraid that if I let the air release, then my inhibitions would be freed. My gut told me anger would only make the situation worse. I hid my feelings. After all, I was an expert at it.

"I'll have you know. Those two were making quite the commotion." The charge nurse's finger glared at Lovebaby, "So I separated them. I am in charge. I can do what I see fit."

To be quite honest that's the stupidest thing I've ever heard. But I did not say that to her face.
"So that's what this is about? Talking? That's all? So, they were talking a little bit? No one else is awake. If anything, you're the one making the commotion. Soon the whole ward will be awake with the drama you have stirred."

An obvious light bulb moment hit her in the face. Obviously, she was too proud to admit anything but her mind had suddenly changed. She turned her head to Lovebaby. "If you two are going to settle down for the night, then your little friend can come back. If I hear even so much as a peep, then back to that room she'll go!"

I had won the fight, now I was even more determined not to allow another injustice to occur. I fought with everything in my body. I had conquered every monster of injustice that came along on an hourly basis.

Sadly, I failed to defeat the evil doctor, the final boss. He may have been a hero to some, but he was the villain in my story. He relocated us, uprooting us from our friends. He threatened to force pills down my throat; even, after I stated that my patient rights declared that I could deny medication at any time.

The evil doctor was some kind of creature I imagined crawled its way up form hell. To this day, I regret not being able to defeat him. I had so desperately wanted to take him on in battle so I could bring justice for him hurting me.

One day, I will come back, to that hospital. Come
back to those White Walls.

The first thing I'll change is those White Walls.

Then, I will modernize staff to listen, empathize,
and respect their patients. I will.

9 780937 176016